I0630141

NO GOOD DEED

NO GOOD DEED

ALSO BY JANUARY BAIN

City of Lies

NO GOOD DEED

JANUARY BAIN

ROUGH
EDGES
PRESS

No Good Deed
Paperback Edition
Copyright © 2024 January Bain

Rough Edges Press
An Imprint of Wolfpack Publishing
701 S. Howard Ave. 106-324
Tampa, FL 33609

roughedgespress.com

This book is a work of fiction. Any references to historical events, real
people or real places are used fictitiously. Other names, characters,
places and events are products of the author's imagination, and any
resemblance to actual events, places or persons, living or dead, is
entirely coincidental.

All rights reserved. No part of this book may be reproduced by any
means without the prior written consent of the publisher, other than
brief quotes for reviews.

Paperback ISBN 978-1-68549-712-5
eBook ISBN 978-1-68549-711-8
LCCN 2024935467

NO GOOD DEED

NO GOOD DEED

PROLOGUE

I'm doing it all over again. A shocking thing that should never be done once in a lifetime, let alone twice. I'm making a body vanish in the dark. And I'm praying like mad my actions will never see the light of day.

As I dig the hole, struggling with the spade to cut into the cement-like soil we call prairie gumbo, I keep asking myself why did it happen again? *Why?* I'd tried so hard to live my life aboveboard since that terrible time nine years ago.

The droning chorus of insects hidden in the trees provide no answer to my mental query. My mind drifts back into the past, reliving a nightmare that never goes away.

It was just before I graduated from high school, finally free to leave my hometown behind, when everything had come tumbling down around me like the famed walls of Jericho. Now I'm all too aware of how guilt eats at you, leeches all the color out of your day. Your life. I've tried to be a good friend, a good wife,

1

helped my family whenever I could, and yet here I am, in a worse situation than the first time it happened.

My thoughts are scattered now, like the disturbed soil laying all around the freshly dug grave. The body is wrapped up, laying still nearby, a testament to my doing what I had to do to survive. My body's tired, dead tired, breaking down, bleeding from the gunshot wound. But I have to persevere, protect those I love until my last dying breath. I swipe at the sweat beads breaking out on my forehead, blinking against the sting of salt dripping in my eyes.

Who should I blame? A young woman thinking she can change a man for the better? The foster system throwing innocents to the wolves long before they're ready because they aged out? Or the whole of society for allowing abuse behind closed doors and not appearing to give a damn?

No, I blame me.

My spade hits another rock left over from the last ice age, jarring my entire body. I can only hope my wound doesn't open up again. I have to ignore the burning pain in my side which is growing more insistent with each movement, each memory, echoing the one lodged in my heart.

False dawn is about to arrive in the east and I know I must hurry this along. But my mind stays focused on memories of another night, so eerily similar to this one it defied the odds. I can still smell the stench of bodily fluids, see the dark waters of the fast-flowing Red River, and hear the sounds of the body splashing into the cold depths before disappearing forever below the oily surface.

What's the most important thing to have in life? I've asked myself the question many times since that fateful day that forever changed my world. When I was with my husband, it was security, to be kept hidden safe and sound, removed from the world. And look how that turned out. It was a fantasy, an unrealistic life that collapsed around us all too soon, with my secrets pushing him away and into the arms of another woman. Or at least that's how he tells it.

When I'm with my best friend, it's to support each other, to have a place to weather the inevitable storms of life, have a mutual understanding. Respect.

And when I'm alone, without anyone to focus on, my greatest need is for courage. The courage to forgive myself.

CHAPTER 1
KATIE

TWENTY HOURS EARLIER—MONDAY 8 A.M.

You're supposed to forgive and forget.

If you asked most people, you do the hard work of forgiving to get rewarded with peace of mind. Forgiving them makes you a better person, helps set you free, *yada yada*.

I stopped fighting with the blasted wool that kept shredding under my twitchy fingers, throwing my current therapy project away from me with disgust. Counting stitches this morning to finish the crocheted afghan I'd promised my sister Rose had proved impossible. Normally, I enjoyed applying the skill my grandmother had taught me as a child, finding it relaxing. Not today.

What was going on across the street?

I lived in a small cul-de-sac of only a handful of homes, a much-coveted location with great neighbors and an even better view. I'd bought Riverbend, my dream home, when I first made it big in the gaming software industry. The spacious lot and acres of riverfront were hard to come by in a city, even a small city, a relic of another age when elegance won out over greed.

Riverbend was my sanctuary, especially since I'd become a single divorced woman living alone. The manor-style limestone house was so huge even the helpful real estate agent had tried to talk me out of buying it, what with its six bedrooms, five bathrooms, and a swimming pool. Most people would think it far too large, but I loved it. One day every bedroom would be filled, they could mark my words. I'd been trying to get my sister Rose to move in with her children, but so far, no dice.

A ping on my cell phone riveted my attention away from the worry about the new neighbors and Rose's situation, but spotting the number of my ex made me groan out loud.

Brad Bennett
Decided to take Andy on vaycay so you're off the hook. 😊

The happy face added at the end of the text was too much and I had to bite back the tears. The bastard. I had been counting on two weeks alone with my furry baby. The border cross collie had stolen my heart during our short-lived marriage. I missed Andy's presence in my life more than my ex, ten to one.

To take my mind off my grief and refusing to beg Brad because from long experience I knew it wouldn't work to try to convince him of letting me have Andy, I decided to head out for my usual morning jog. Hey, I'd have gotten on my knees and pleaded my case with my ex if I stood half a chance of changing his passive aggressive stance. Never going to happen.

I jumped up from the sofa and eased the living room drape back just enough to check the street. My eyes flicked back and forth, checking out everything I could see. All clear. Last thing I wanted was to run into the new neighbors' house sitting for Daniel Johnson, a man I liked and admired. Ashley was fine, but Quinton Riley begged the question of why some women are with bad boys. All tattoos and attitude. This one even rode a Harley motorcycle, the sight and sound of which made my stomach fold in on itself. Memories crept in like phantoms in the mist. I squelched them with extreme prejudice. The keeping of secrets was essential to my continuing the good life, hundreds of kilometers from the small northern town in Canada I'd grown up in.

Casper, Manitoba, Canada. Known for the town mascot of, wait for it, a ghost. So far no one had been sued over it, but maybe it's because the ghost wasn't cute, but rather generic, though it did feature a rather friendly smile. I was never certain it fit. Casper was not known for accepting outsiders. I would've known. I watched firsthand what the new kid on the block went through on their way to trying to be accepted. Maybe if we'd all been nicer to Wyatt Draeger a little sooner none of this would have happened. Sadie would be unscarred. Josie would still be alive. Actually, that sign should've been changed to a dark apparition with glowing red eyes in its skull. A much more accurate representation.

I unlocked the triple dead bolts, one by one. *Try taking a bump key or an electric drill to this many*, I silently shouted at a possible robber. Each one clicked loudly as the stiff bullet-shaped steel was pulled out of its thick slot by a twist of my determined fingers. Overkill, but essential, like the safe room hidden between my office and one of the downstairs bedrooms, my number one reason for buying this place. Taking a deep breath, I slipped out the front door, keeping a sharp eye out for any telltale movement. I dallied on the front steps, pretending to tie my running shoe, then stretched various muscle groups while darting furtive looks across the street. No worrying sounds or activities.

Okay then.

Already dressed in my running gear and prepared for a three-mile hike, I headed off down the street. Breakfast sat like a rock in my stomach, making me regret eating anything, though it was just a piece of toast. I needed this activity enough to put up with the anxiety and stress, the worry tightening my throat for it would pass at some point during my run. I needed to make peace with this latest arrow piercing my heart from my ex.

I hadn't been out in two days, not since the pair had moved in across the street. I greedily took the fresh morning air deep into my lungs, enjoying the sense of bestowing some order on my life. I made it to the end of the street leading away from our secluded cul-de-sac without incident and turned to the right, intending to enjoy the reprieve. Beginning to breathe easier, feeling the earth beneath my feet again as solid and firm, I allowed the sense of dread to fall away and slide off my shoulders. It was just what I needed, endorphins crowding out the fog encasing my brain. I'd tossed and turned for two nights, falling into the loop of the old nightmare I'd hoped I'd left behind.

No such luck.

The sudden loud rumble of a motorcycle broke the still of the quiet neighborhood, sending birdsong into instant retreat. Quinton. The guy from across the street who'd kept me from feeling safe enough to go out for a jog these past few days.

I began running quicker, my feet pounding the paved sidewalk. I pulled my hoodie up over my earphones, the universal sign for *leave me the hell alone*. He wouldn't pull anything, right, not in broad daylight with a few passersby out and about? Not that he had done anything to call the police about, at least not yet. It was more the sense of unease being around him created. Dread of the unknown. A panic that was entrenched in my subconscious. It never let loose of my soul, try as I might.

The wall of sound intensified; an assault to the eardrums.

Thud. Thud. Thud.

Why hadn't someone reported him? Probably decided to leave the dirty work to others. I shook my head. The enclave in Tuxedo I'd moved to three years ago was a closed affair, everyone keeping to themselves for the most part, just the way I liked it. Only neighbor I actually talked with was Daniel, and that was rarely. Plus, people were at work again. I had the luxury of still being home after pandemic restrictions had passed, though not much longer if I didn't get my act together. Owning a virtual business had some rewards, though most of them were falling like children's building blocks knocked over by a careless hand at the moment.

The motorcycle pulled up alongside me, the annoying pitch of the engine slowing down to a low stone-throwing rumble offering nothing to ease the situation. He was coming up on my blind side from behind me, making my skin crawl. I continued to ignore him, my heart thumping, and my body producing a slick of sweat at an alarming rate.

It became impossible to avoid an encounter a few seconds later as he revved the powerful engine up to full throttle to gain my attention. The stench of burning gasoline destroyed the fresh air. I slanted my eyes toward him, just in time to catch him flipping me the bird. The image sent me reeling into the past. Ten years earlier, to be precise, to the time another bastard had gotten off doing the same hand action.

Wyatt Draeger. Hometown football hero. Street racer. Abuser of women. When the man on the bike pushed up his visor, it was Wyatt's face that appeared framed by the off-putting too-slick black helmet. His smug grin hid a world of misogyny. Not all his fault, since the apple doesn't fall far from the tree, and was never truer than in this case. His father was still doing a stretch in prison for manslaughter compounded by his actions while incarcerated, having stabbed another prisoner over some perceived insult.

I met Wyatt in high school. His family moving into our neighborhood an unusual attraction in our small town where memories were long and secrets kept buried, only occasionally rising up and creating mayhem. A double homicide of cheating spouses while I was in high school came to mind. Their deaths bore witness to the urgent reason for keeping things hidden when the husband of one of the pairs took the law into his own hands.

But that first day meeting the Draeger family, when I'd gone over to welcome the newcomers with my mother's freshly baked apple pie in hand, he'd met me at the door. I'd stammered my welcome, overwhelmed by his good looks, cool name, and rakish charm uncommon in Casper. If only I'd known then what his arrival would lead to, I'd have dropped that pie and ran. Instead, I'd ended up introducing him to my best friend, Sadie. Biggest mistake of my life. One I would have to live with forever.

"I'm warning you. Stay the hell away from Ashley." Quinton's sour words spilled out of his contorted, angry mug yanking me back from the past.

"Ashley needs a friend," I said in weak protest. Just like Sadie did. I'd failed her; a pain that would never abate. Why hadn't I gotten there sooner?

"Not one who fills her head with nonsense. We're only here for a short time while Thompson's away. Stay clear, if you know what's good for you, ma'am." His rapid words hit like shots fired from a hunting rifle.

I pressed my lips together to prevent the encounter from escalating. Was the *ma'am* meant to disarm me, set me in my place? We looked to be about the same age, twenty-seven, or maybe he was a bit older than me. But I was also confused by his little speech. I could honestly say I hadn't tried to offer Ashley any advice. I'd just met her, for heaven's sake. But his words had confirmed my suspicions, which made him either stupid or dangerous, probably both.

A final grim stare directed at me chilled the marrow in my bones, his gray eyes drilling into me, cold as steel. Then he replaced the helmet that gave him the anonymous look of a futurist hornet, all monstrous edges and looming threats. Gunning the engine, he maneuvered the heavy bike forward, vanishing around the corner in a puff of smoke. I bit my inner lip and the taste of rusty metal flooded my mouth. The disgusting stench of spent fuel filled my nostrils.

I shouldn't get involved. Just point the way to the authorities. *Remember how it turned out last time?* They'd be gone soon anyway. I wasn't certain my body could handle any more stress, let alone my mind. What did they call it? PTSD. Well, whatever. I didn't like labels anyway; they painted you into a corner. But it was the

11

brain protecting itself. A.k.A. survival. But it had been in part responsible for destroying my marriage. Working on myself at this point might be too late to save my relationship, but perhaps it could help create a better future. But not if I got myself involved in something that was not my affair. Not minding my own business was courting disaster. But maybe I was her only hope? Maybe she wouldn't seek help without me pushing her toward it?

My heart pinged with concern for the young woman. I'd been considered the one most likely in high school to become a social worker. I snorted. I was a long way from that reality, having created a well-received computer app for a new relationship gaming experience: *Lovecupid*. Easiest way I knew to stay safe, keep your romantic life online. Not to mention, the guarantee of a virtual hookup beat real world rejection anytime.

My best bet, my current therapist would've advised, was to keep a low profile. The couple across the street would soon be gone, taking their drama with them, Ashley shared they were housesitting while Daniel Johnson was in Rome. Daniel had surprised me there, as usually one of his relatives stayed at his place while he spent time abroad. This time he'd taken in strangers for hire. Odd, but maybe no one in his family was available on short notice. Usually, he mentioned his itinerary, or at least the fact he was going out of town. But this time the whole transaction of his leaving and the new pair moving in had happened without my prior knowledge. Ashley and I had exchanged phone numbers, so this did have the look of being on the up and up. But something was making me uncomfortable. I made a note to look into it.

I resumed my run, chewing over the short conversation I'd had with Ashley two days ago. It was in the eyes, the insecurity, the hesitation, the defensive words even as the bright sunlight showed to glaring effect the makeup on her cheek meant to hide the bruising. Then Quinton had pushed his way between us, acting the big man and saying they had to be some place. *Like right f-ing now.*

Well, Ashley did have a choice. There were services available to help her. I just needed to catch her alone and have a talk with her without Quinton around. He was blaming me anyway, so might as well try to approach her. That much I could do at least, even if making the effort here did drag up the pain I'd worked hard to suppress with copious amounts of alcohol. But I was doing better of late, slowing my consumption of vodka. I could ill afford the lost productive time it brought on. Maybe I could discover a new idea for an app. I remembered the charge of adrenaline the creation process always gave me. The money I'd made from *Lovecupid* wasn't going to last forever, not the way Rose and her family were tearing through it. And Sadie needed my help just as much, unable to work with the lingering effects of the abuse at the hands of someone who promised to love and cherish her for the rest of her life. I'd helped her change her last name and hide her identity so no one from her past could ever find her.

But the last thing I wanted was something to set off those negative voices again. The ones saying I wasn't good enough, smart enough, or pretty enough. Unfortunately, they also knew the truth of it as well as I do. I was a fake. I probably just hid it better than most.

CHAPTER 2
ASHLEY

I peeked out the window, keeping a sharp eye on the house across the street. I'd met the woman who lived there when Quinton and I moved in. Katie Kelly. Like I could conjure her up, the front door opened and she appeared on her front step wearing running gear.

She was the only neighbor I'd met so far. She'd taken it upon herself to come over and introduce herself. If only Quinton hadn't come out right then, I might have spent some time with her, gotten to know her. I bit all around my thumbnail, tearing a strip of skin clear off. The pain was immediate and brough a wash of tears to my eyes I blinked away. At least it was a torment I caused myself.

I heard Quinton's bike start up in the attached garage, the distinctive vroom-vroom thrumming in my veins. I hated that bike and everything it stood for. It was what had brought us together in a moment of shared passion for flouting the rules.

When he swung the hog out onto the street to follow in the same direction as our neighbor, I ducked back out of view. *Please don't let him be harassing her.* It would be like him though. Always had to be seen as the tough guy. He even had me call him by his nickname when we were alone, Top Dog. Silly stupid name.

He'd been a minor contender in his wrestling division back in college *and don't you forget it. Phttt.*

Of course, he had his good points, I thought, reminding myself to calm down. He found decent housesitting jobs that kept a roof over our heads. And he'd acquired some good connections over the past year that offered opportunities for our business. That was something else I was never supposed to talk about, the kind of business we were in, if I knew what was good for me. Still, he did what he had to survive, same as any man would do if pushed to the wall, right? I couldn't be with a wimp, someone who couldn't help provide, no matter his lot in life or his bad beginning. I'd overcome a horrible upbringing I wouldn't wish on my worst enemy. And yet I was still standing, trying to become better.

That reminded me of the list. I pulled the folded sheet of paper from my pocket Quinton had me write in my own handwriting this morning and reread it out loud.

"Ashley's Self-Improvement List:

Never let anyone know any details about us.

Don't talk back to the Top Dog.

Always smile when you're with the Top Dog.

Be a perfect girlfriend for the Top Dog.

If the Top Dog asks for a drink, bring him one quick with a smile.

Remember you're nothing without me.

I don't know why I tell you these things because you never change…"

Tears filled my eyes and I swiped at them. *Could I do this, make it work?* I chewed on another ragged cuticle, imagining all kinds of scenarios for this playing out. My job. Putting stuff in the right place, under the best light possible. But I didn't have a crystal ball telling me how to figure things *before* they happened. Well, I just had to work at not taking the list too personally. It was only meant to help me after all. I blinked away another wash of tears and concentrated on what I should work on first. Read a book, finish grade twelve, or get my hair done?

CHAPTER 3
KATIE

MONDAY 9 A.M.

As I stepped from the shower, my phone rang. I reached over and grabbed it off the counter. Dripping wet, I stared at the screen. Rose. What did my older sister want now? We'd talked a couple of days ago and I'd sent her a big bundle of my dwindling cash.

"Hey, sis. What's up?" I asked, pulling a towel off the stack, and wrapping it around myself while holding the phone.

"Just wanted to say I got the money."

Of course, no thanks were attached and were not necessary. We were family, and that's what family does; helps out during the bad times. It seemed Rose's life was always stuck on difficult if not downright complicated. Guilt struck for how much easier I had it, having left town while my older sister had gotten herself pregnant right before graduation. Three kids on a waitress's salary and a husband always between jobs had happened to her in the last nine years since I'd left Casper. They lived in a fire trap of a trailer I was always giving Rose a hard time about so she would find a better place to rent, but she insisted unless I was made of money, it was all she could afford right now. Even when I did send more cash there always seemed to be a greater need than new accommodations.

"Great. Now you can breathe a little easier, right?" It was impossible to dry myself on the phone and I gave up on the process. I would try to keep the call short and sweet. Other things were pressing at me that needed doing today. Ashley's bruised face rose up in my mind. She was too thin. And tiny. That big brute had been manhandling her, I was certain of it. Otherwise, why warn me to stay away? The idiot had given the game away without realizing it.

"Well, here's the thing..." The slight hesitation made my gut roil. *Oh-oh*. Now what? Paying for Meghan's new braces and the antiquated plumbing and electrical system had cleared me out of available funds I'd allotted for this month, meaning I was already dipping into next month's allotment.

"That used car you bought me died on my way to work yesterday and the mechanic down at Casper Motors said it was going to need a lot of labor to make it roadworthy again."

How did she manage to make it sound like it was my bad which had caused her car issues? Like I was the one held responsible for not buying her a new vehicle even though my own vehicle was a few years old? Paying for a divorce from my ex who was unfortunately a lawyer with good connections had about broken the bank.

"How much?" I asked with a sigh I couldn't quite keep inside, try as I might.

"Can't you create one of those little apps or something?" Rose's voice got that edge that made me wince with guilt while she disparaged the process. I had led her on, bragging about how on the app had been so exhilarating to create and had brought a ready pile of cash with it. But it wasn't like I could pull them out of thin air.

"It takes time, Rose." I pressed the palm of my hand against my hot forehead, feeling the beginnings of a migraine begin to take hold. A flash of lights behind my closed eyelids confirmed my diagnosis.

"Well, it's not like you're not good for it, right? I need the car. It's my only way to get to work. Joe has to have his truck to get around during the day, to look for jobs." No point in asking Joe to be inconvenienced in any way. We'd had that discussion before and it never went well.

"How about the bus? Just until the end of the month?"

"The bus? Lining up with all those degenerates. No way. There was an incident a few weeks back. This guy —he pulls a knife on the driver. Do you want to put me in harm's way? I got three little kids. You don't understand what it's like."

"Of course I don't want anything to happen to you! I'll find a way. Give me a day or two." Maybe I could hock some jewelry? I had a couple of nice pieces left. Just, they'd been given to me by our grandmother and I hated the thought of them sitting in a pawnshop while I found the cash to get them back. I might have to consider selling my home. Now that Brad had moved out, my finances were dwindling at too fast a rate. But the idea only brought on more panic. Without my safe harbor, how could I exist? No, I'd starve, work my fingers to the bone, rather than lose Riverbend.

"I have to let the mechanic know right away because he needs to order parts. And he said he requires a down payment for those. Rip-off, I know. But I need the car so what am I supposed to do?"

Which credit card could take the hit? I'd been playing Russian roulette with my finances of late, promising myself I'd sort it out soon.

"How much does he need?"

"Eight-fifty."

I rubbed my forehead again, trying to will the pain away. I must call the pharmacy and refill my prescription.

"Okay. Give me his number and I'll okay the purchase on a credit card."

The doorbell rang as Rose gave over the details.

"I gotta go. Someone's at the door."

"Okay. Don't forget. Like that time when I needed—"

I cut her off. "I was right in the middle of an important launch for the app. I made it up to you the next day soon as I remembered." Why is it you can do something good for someone more times than you can count, but miss once, and that seems to be all they can remember? Was it a universal human failure? Focusing on the bad over the good. But who was I to talk. I often focused on the negative over the positive.

"But not before Joe Junior cried himself to sleep over not having the money to go on the overnight school trip with his friends. Probably why he's gotten a bit out of hand these days. Did you know I caught him smoking out behind our place?"

I bit my lip. "I'm sorry about it, okay. I sent him the Xbox to make up for it. I needed a little more advance notice." I had mentioned the importance of the day for me weeks ahead, not that my sister ever listened to my needs.

"We should plan our days around your schedule?"

I took a deep breath. My sister had a bad habit of always being on the defensive around me. Most likely my fault. I should be more considerate of her feelings. Not like she enjoyed calling me and asking for money.

The doorbell chimed again, giving me the needed excuse to end the stalemate. "I'm not saying that. Look, I gotta go. Someone's at the door."

"Sure. Whatever. Just don't forget."

The phone went dead in my ear. Why did Rose always do that? Make it sound like I'm lying when I'm not?

Annoyed, I yanked my robe off the hook and thrust my arms through the sleeves, tying it tightly around my waist. Heck, I had been losing weight, noticing how much of the tie hung down. Throwing my hair up into a towel, I raced from the bathroom to answer the door.

I checked through the peephole, surprised to see Ashley standing there holding a baking dish in her hands. Without a second of hesitation, I pulled the three deadbolts and unlocked the door.

Her eyes looking too big for her face, she thrust the pie plate at me.

"Hope you like apple pie?"

In point of fact, it was the only kind of dessert I never, ever ate. But I squelched down my unease at the memory and reached out to take it from her. Wyatt Draeger would always be associated with apple pie. I couldn't choke down a piece voluntarily if my life depended on it. All American or not.

"Thanks. That's very kind of you. But you didn't have to do that. It's me who should be welcoming you to the neighborhood with pastry." Why hadn't I done that already? I guess because their arrival had been unexpected. And of course, they weren't going to be around for long. I didn't normally offer baked goods to the relatives who stayed in Daniel's house short term.

Her pale skin pinked. She looked better today, if far too thin. Her hair was freshly washed, so she was trying to make a good appearance. Her skin devoid of makeup, she looked too innocent to be with the man across the street though she appeared to be the about the same age as me. She'd be pretty if not for the bruise marring her cheek that appeared to be fading.

"It's okay. I like to bake."

I stepped back, holding the still warm pie. "Would you like to come in?"

"You just got out of the shower. I should go."

"Nonsense." What if this was my only chance to talk some sense into her? She'd mentioned they were only here for a week. "You're not interrupting at all. Come in. I'll put some coffee on."

Ignoring the pain pounding at my skull like a merciless drummer, I led the way through the living room into the kitchen.

"Wow. That's some artwork hanging on the walls."

"Thanks."

"Is that a Warhol?"

Ashley stood rooted in front of the first real treasure my money had brought me, other than this house and my over-the-top wedding to Brad, the uber commercial real estate lawyer who needed to impress his friends and make senior partner. Note to self, next time, if there is a next time, keep it simple. I had collected a few nice pieces of art over the years though, but this one was special. Too bad about what I'd had to do. The memory made my stomach fold in on itself again.

"Yes, but it's not worth millions. It's only an early screen print." I clamped my mouth shut. And now a fake, something I hated to admit. The original had been sold to pay for the divorce. Brad had come after me with guns blazing, knowing the best way to hurt me after I'd hurt him with demanding a divorce after he'd cheated, was to make me sell it, and split the profits. And worse yet, he had taken Andy, our furry baby, a border cross collie that had captured my heart. Though Brad had brought Andy to the marriage, the loving dog had taken to me far more as his companion, running alongside me and spending far more time with me than Brad.

But at least I was still entrenched in the family home christened Riverbend by the former owners, lonely as all get out, but the only place I could be safe. My saving grace, I'd bought the coveted house with my own money before the marriage, my name being the only one on the deed. Brad got the lake house, which was worth nearly as much, though certainly not as prestigious an address as Riverbend. My headache bloomed with the memory of the fights with him, the incriminating words, darkening the edges of my vision. Maybe now was not the time to speak with Ashley? I was under a lot of stress already today and it was still early.

"Still, I mean, everyone knows who he is, right?"

"Hmm." I swallowed, trying to wish the headache away. I had to do this. This might be my only chance.

"Ashley…"

"You have such a nice place. You're so lucky. I'll bet your husband's a great guy too." Her wishful expression broke my heart.

"He was."

"Oh, I'm sorry." Ashley began chewing on her fingernail, drawing my attention to what bad shape her hands were in, all red and raw around the edges of her cuticles.

23

You got this. I filled my lungs, forcing myself to stay in the moment.

"That's okay. Divorce is fairly common these days."

"Doesn't make it hurt any less when it's your own, right?" The sympathy in Ashley's expression didn't quite make it to her eyes.

"No, that's all too true."

I continued walking toward the kitchen, certain she would follow. I'd prepared the coffee maker earlier and only had to switch it on.

"Would you like some pie?" I asked. *Please say no.*

"Sure." Ashley chose a stool under the counter and sat down, watching me.

After pulling two plates from the cupboard, I dutifully cut into the cursed pie and placed a piece on each. Of course, the expensive silver engraved pie server dripped juice onto the counter. Ignoring it, I opened a drawer and picked out two forks, setting one in front of her on a cloth napkin.

"Thanks." She gave me a bright smile. I recognized the look when it only involved the lower part of her face. Some women living in a bad situation try too hard.

I poured two cups of coffee, and I sat down beside her at the counter and pointed out the sugar bowl.

"Do you take cream?"

"No, but thanks." She added two heaping teaspoons of sugar to her mug, stirring it. She hesitated, like she wasn't certain where to put the wet spoon.

"The counter's washable," I said.

She set down the spoon and picked up the fork, taking a bite of pie. "Yum. Apple's my favorite. One of the few things I bake well. Even Quinton says so and he's, well, he's got high standards." She eyed me sideways. "You're not hungry?"

"Not really. But it does smell delicious."

I can do this. I didn't want to disappoint her. I took a small bite. It didn't taste like homemade, far more like tinned apple and soggy piecrust. Was she lying about making it? Why would she do that? It didn't make any sense. Maybe she wanted to impress me, and this was her lame attempt as she was a poor cook. Not like I hadn't exaggerated on occasion. But then, don't we all.

Dark spots swam in tight circles across my vision. Right. Get on with it.

"So, how long have you and Quinton been together?"

"Long time; since I turned eighteen. We intend to make it legal soon. Just been too busy. But he's been helping me so-o much. I gotta lot to learn. I'm not good at things."

"Like what?" I took a few sips of the excellent hot, black coffee. Caffeine sometimes helped my headaches. I felt it ease with the suggestion.

She shrugged her thin shoulders, chewing at her bottom lip thoughtfully. "Like a lot of things. Quinton's so good at stuff, he points out what I'm doing wrong. I'm working real hard to correct myself."

"You know you're already good enough, right? You're a beautiful, articulate young woman who appreciates fine art. He's lucky to be with someone like you. Don't ever apologize for who you are, Ashley." I launched into it, needing to get to the heart of the matter. Quickly. My body was balking at not lying down, ready to crash underneath me. I had few precious moments to say what I needed, desperation having set in. I wanted this young woman to be okay, to walk away if the situation warranted it. All signs pointed in that direction.

"Well, there's lots of room for improvement, right?" she said, her mouth flattened.

"But only what *you* choose to be important. Not what someone else forces on you."

She flushed. "He doesn't force me. I ask for it."

"You ask for what exactly?" I inquired very, very softly.

Her lips twitched and her hand went up to cup her cheek. *Yeah, right, that kind of correction.*

"There's help if you need it." I reached for the business card I'd dug out earlier and handed it to her. "These people will help you day or night, no questions asked."

She struck down the lifeline like I had burned her, knocking my hand aside.

"It's not like that, okay? I gotta go." She jumped to her feet and raced from the room, spilling her coffee and dumping the pie on the counter in the process.

I threw a dishtowel over the mess and raced after her.

"Ashley, it's okay. I understand. Just so you know, I have a safe room if you ever need it."

She turned a tear-stained face my way, having yanked open the front door. "You understand nothing, okay! Leave me the hell alone!"

"Ashley!" I called after her, making my head feel like it was about to split wide open and spill my brains all over the cement. "I'm sorry. Okay? Come back."

I watched her slight figure race across the front lawn like a long-legged colt, her dark curtain of hair a flag waving behind her. If only I knew then what I came to know later, I could have stopped everything in its tracks right then and there.

CHAPTER 4
ASHLEY

"What did that bitch have to say for herself?" Quinton swung around from glaring out the window to face me, his fists clenched by his side. Quinton outweighed me by a good ninety pounds, looming over me at every opportunity. He got a charge out of it. The guy needed an off and on switch. Maybe AI was the way to go? Making Quinton into a robot would have advantages. Safer, and I could call the shots. Make all the rules. But right now, he was helping me for a change, I had to focus on that.

"She was nice. Invited me in for coffee. Normal stuff." I averted my eyes. Like some caged animal, he didn't like to be stared at directly. Anxiety made my body tremble as the adrenaline high vanished. It had been a close call with Katie. I'd only held on to myself by a slim margin.

His dark eyes narrowed, his nostrils flaring wide. I knew the look all too well. Someone better look out.

"I have a good mind to go over there right now and tell that bitch a thing or two," he growled, his stance menacing.

"We're going to be here for a few more days. There's no need to push things."

"Yeah, whatever. Just remember without me, babe, this all goes up in smoke. I need a beer."

I didn't mention the time of day, knowing better. Just scurried off to the kitchen to take care of it. *Keep cool, Ashley, it's only a little while longer*, I reminded myself as I pulled a can of Coors Light from the refrigerator.

When I handed Quinton his beer, he held on to my wrist, his fingers digging into the sensitive flesh.

"You haven't shared what you found out about the joint yet," he said.

I tried pulling my arm away, but he hung on, squeezing tighter until I thought the bones would crack.

"Please stop, you're hurting me. And you're going to like what I have to say. I promise."

He nodded and let go, chugging back half the can, legs spread wide. Aggressive as hell. "I'd better. Go ahead. What's the bitch hiding?"

Soon this would be over, I promised myself as I rubbed my offended wrist to ease the pain. Keep the end date in mind. I'd be out of here so fast his head would twist right off. But I wanted retribution first. *Be careful of what you've done, karma can be a bitch, people.* I launched into my intel.

"Expensive paintings worth a fortune. Even an Andy Warhol. And we know she has jewelry. That first day when she came over, she was wearing a gorgeous neck-lace with a huge tear-drop shaped emerald surrounded by diamonds. Sure, the setting was old-fashioned, but aren't antiques all the rage now?"

His eyes narrowed as he finished his beer, like he suspected I wasn't telling him everything. Did anyone ever tell someone everything? Did he think I was crazy?

"Anything else I should know, babe?"

I broadened my smile with determination, trying to appear as innocent as possible. "Big screen, real silverware. I didn't get a chance to check out her bedroom." I thought of how I ran away from Katie who only wanted to help me. Why had I done that? It had been the perfect opportunity. Not like she didn't suspect anyway. *Phttt*. No way. Why would she help me, an unknown, a nobody, that didn't make a lick of sense.

"You're slipping. You usually do better than that."

"I'll make it up to you, I promise. But first, I gotta feed and water the guy. If he dies, this whole thing changes from robbery to murder. You don't want that, right?"

"A day or two without food's not going to kill the guy."

"But lack of water can." I chewed on a non-existent fingernail.

"Stop that. You know I hate it. You don't have to pretend around me, babe."

Yes, I do. "I won't take but a couple of minutes, Top Dog," I said as sweetly as possible. I never knew what would set him off. An ounce of flattery might prevent it.

"Okay." He gave a wave like a king on a throne.

Generous of you, making sure a man doesn't die.

His next words made my pulse ratchet up. "I've decided on a change in plans. We go in tonight. In case she has other ideas and leaves town."

"Tonight? I thought we agreed giving it a day or two."

"Each hour increases the risk. What if a relative with a key to the house drops by? Ever think of that?"

I chewed on my bottom lip. Once Quinton's mind was made up there was no changing it. And he had a good point. The longer we stayed, the more risk we took.

"I'll be back shortly." I tore off to the kitchen, picking up the mask off the table, then taking the stairs two at a time down to the basement.

A series of low moans emanating from the corner sent relief sluicing through me. At least he was still alive. The amount of ketamine Quinton had dosed Johnson with had me worried. A hard knock on the head followed by ketamine, the hallucinogenic or date rape drug couldn't be good for anybody. I should know, I'd once been tricked into drinking a beer containing the illegal substance myself. I'd been in terrible shape for days, struggling with my memory loss, trying to make sense of things.

Hardening my expression, I approached the owner of the house with caution. *Just because a person looks too out of it to hurt you, don't make it true.*

CHAPTER 5
KATIE

MONDAY 10:30 A.M.

My phone pinged with an incoming text. *Sadie*.

Sadie
Where are u?

Me
Home.

Did u forget?

What was she talking about? I blinked. Realization hit followed by a tsunami of crushing guilt. With all the drama of the past two days I had completely forgotten what day it was. Shame streaked through me.

I sent a text with trembling fingers to say I was on my way before rushing to dress in a somber outfit and find my car keys. How could I forget the anniversary of Josie's death?

Rushing into the attached garage, I hit the button on

my visor to raise the door and jumped into my Tesla. Backing into the street, I glanced across the road and caught a glimpse of a small, pale face peering out the window before the drape was yanked back into place. No time to think of what was going on inside the house. My best friend should not have to face this day alone. I couldn't feel worse than if the Almighty himself had me answering for my crimes.

A memory of Wyatt Draeger flitted across my mind as I drove the thirty minutes to Forest Lawn Cemetery. I thought back to the day Sadie told me he was the man she was going to marry.

"Look, isn't it the best!" Sadie gushed as she held out her left hand with the engagement ring circling the finger.

"Really? But you're about to graduate and we planned to go off to college together."

Her eyes narrowed. "Are you jealous or something? Plans change all the time. Wyatt says I can take night classes right in Casper or distance ed through RRC. Why go away only to return? I can't wait to get a job; I need to start saving up for the wedding."

Because I need to get you as far away from him as I can?

I never trusted Wyatt, not after he had drunk too much one night when everyone was partying out at the quarry pit and he got mad or jealous about something and he'd struck Sadie. He'd been all over her to apologize, sending notes and flowers for days, making a big deal of never doing it again, that he'd rather cut off his own hand. After looking like she was going to wake up and learn the error of her ways, she'd relented one night. Ever since, there had been this slight strain between us, Sadie always on the defensive and no longer sharing every little detail about them.

Was that the seed for what happened later? His jealousy

over another male daring to look Sadie's way? That night in the quarry, Sadie hadn't been exactly herself, flirting with Ian Ross, something out of character for her. But everyone knew Ian. And it was just harmless stuff. There is never any excuse for hitting another person, not if you say you love them or not. Walk away first.

The turn off for Forest Lawn came into view, and I signaled with my turning light before entering the wrought-iron gates. Baby Josie Mary Katherine Draeger's grave was near the back of the graveyard, the newest section, and not yet shaded by a canopy of trees. I pulled up at the curb behind Sadie's used Toyota Prius Eco. When I got out of my vehicle the stillness of the place washed over me; it became oppressive with a sense of being hushed and in another dimension. I spotted Sadie fifty yards away across the greenscape, her head bowed. I still wasn't used to her black, choppy locks. Sadie had been a long-haired, golden-blonde growing up, back when I knew her as Merri. But it was a good disguise. She looked nothing like that golden girl now.

My low heels sunk into the newly clipped grass, the fragrance sharp, and making me sneeze. The sound was too loud for the space and I tried to stifle the second sneeze, blowing up my sinuses. A third one had my eyes watering and my nose dripping. I checked the pocket of my dress for a tissue and found nothing but lint. I sniffed and wiped my nose on the back of my hand.

When I got close to Sadie she glanced my way, her eyes reddened by weeping. I wrapped my arms around her and held her close for a while, until a car horn barked and she pulled away.

"Sorry I'm late."

"That's okay. You didn't have to come."

"I wanted to come." At that moment I wished I'd

33

stopped to pick up flowers, but the desperate need to get to my friend as soon as possible had overcome me and I hadn't thought to stop along the way.

Sadie had already laid a new bouquet of Baby's Breath and pale pink tea roses on the small grave, underneath the 3D image of an angel with spread wings with the inscription I've read many times. Yet it never failed to bring tears to my eyes. Today was no exception.

JOSIE MARY KATHERINE DRAEGER

July 18th, 2015–July 19th, 2015.

Beloved daughter, granddaughter.

Called home by the angels. Mommy will always love you.

Sleep in peace little one.

I placed my arm around Sadie's slender shoulders, tugging her close. We stood side by side, remembering, both of us consumed by the past. Was she racked by the same weight of guilt as me? No, it was me that should have been there sooner.

Sadie gave out a long sigh, unable to keep the accusation out of her voice. "How could you forget?"

The question set me off balance. She had the right to ask. After all that had happened, it would seem an impossible challenge to forget the events leading up to the tragedy for a single second.

"A couple moved in across the street," I began, trying to make sense of it myself.

"Did Daniel sell the place?"

"No, just a pair housesitting while he's away." Why hadn't I tried to contact Daniel yet to confirm their story? Something was off about them, stuck in my gut like a coil of writhing snakes, but maybe it was the past coloring the present. Not the first time I'd overreacted to a couple's suspected situation. I tried a bit harder to keep a lower profile now, not wanting the unnecessary attention of law enforcement. My past was too checkered to bear scrutiny. Same as Sadie's.

"And?"

"She looks—Ashley that is—to be maybe a victim of spousal abuse."

"Oh Lord, did you talk to her?" I had her attention now, and I sensed the recoil inside my friend's rail-thin body.

"They just moved in two days ago and will be gone within the week. But yes, I did. Gave her a card for the right people to call. She didn't take it well."

"You got to try again. Maybe if I talk to her?" Sadie pressed; her eyes luminous with emotion.

"Maybe? Are you sure you're up for it? Today's been a hard day. It might be too much dealing with issues like that." A sliver of hope stirred. Maybe the perspective of a woman who had lost everything due to one man would be the thing to persuade Ashley?

"I need something to take my mind off things. And if I can prevent one woman from being harmed, it can only help, right?" Sadie stood up taller, pushing her shoulders back with determination. There was the old Sadie, the one I'd grown up with pre-Wyatt Draeger.

"Why don't you come over for dinner? I'll invite her and maybe we can talk with her, help her? That's if she'll come?" I gave a negative shake of my head. "She was pretty angry earlier today. Ran off screaming to leave her the hell alone."

"Tell her you're making your famous lasagna and she'll be over in a flash."

"It's summer and it's going to be a scorcher. I'm

thinking more along the lines of a salad and grilled salmon."

"Ply her with alcohol, she's more likely to open up."

I shook my head. "I can't do that in good conscience. It's the kind of thing a guy would do to get his way."

"Better us than an abusive asshole getting his hands on her again." Sadie's tone hardened, her lips flattening. She seldom swore, but this was easily forgivable.

I nodded. "Okay. I'll try to arrange it."

The sense of a clock ticking quicker and louder in my brain made me antsy to leave, the quiet of the graveyard only serving to enhance the sensation. Why did I feel like something was in play that could not be stopped? Something that would be catastrophic to someone? *Get a grip, Katie, you can't know that for certain.*

But I'd had the sensation once before, back just before Sadie's baby girl died. A terrible turning point to our lives that had caused things to happen that could never be undone. The horrid secret Sadie and I shared, bonded us for life. I didn't want to add anything else on the negative side of the karma sheet before I left this world. But I couldn't stay clear of it either. Bloody catch 22 situations abound in life, at least for me, doomed either way.

CHAPTER 6
ASHLEY

I adjusted my clown mask in futile efforts to see better out of the eyeholes and set the bottle of water and granola bars down on the floor next to the mattress Daniel Johnson lay upon. His hands were tied in front of him with a long cord attached to the overhead black PVC pipe that carried refuse from the toilets down the drain to the sewer system. One leg was chained to one bottom leg of the refrigerator. Quinton wasn't taking any chances. The man's eyes looked stressed above the gag and I frowned, shoving back against the unwanted sympathy for his plight.

"Don't worry. You stay put and no one will hurt you. You'll be free in a few hours anyway. We're almost done here." My reassurance had some effort, the man stopped struggling and moaning, giving me his rapt attention.

"I'm going to loosen your hands, okay, but don't try anything. All I have to do is scream and help will arrive. Then you're in for it. Trust me, you don't want the man upstairs to get angry. You know he's got a gun."

Without warning, the past leered up, exposing its

ugliness to view. *One of my foster mothers had been a real piece of work. Usually, it's the husband, but not this time. I was used to getting into trouble for some things I'd done to earn it, but to be ambushed for no reason was difficult to swallow.*

"Take your clothes off now!" the woman had screamed, her face red, and her eyes bulging, the memory of her unattractive face far too clear in my brain.

It was the dead of winter, but that didn't matter. Susan and I peeled off our clothes. Please don't let it be a wallowing. Water running over bare flesh when its below zero doesn't bear mentioning. Only thing I can say, it toughens you up after the pain passes.

The irate woman pointed at the back door. "Out! The two of you."

Had her other too-perfect daughter pointed fingers to gain us punishment? It would be like her to do that. Strangely, she treated Susan as bad as me, the foster kid. I'd asked Susan about it once, but she only mumbled something about better to have family than not. Better than nothing. I'd challenged that. I'd planned to be on my own soon as I turned of age.

"She's crazy. I hate her," I'd whispered to Susan on our way to the backyard. We could be stuck out there for hours. It had happened before. There was no point in telling the social worker. Susan's mother had her in the palm of her hand while I had too many strikes against me. It was only a few more weeks until my eighteenth anyway. Surely, I could last. I was happy in the school at least. One teacher had even praised one of my drawings. First time that had ever happened.

Soon as Susan and I were out of earshot, we began to play our favorite game: killing her mom, while we stood back-to-back as ordered in the snow-covered field up against the fence. The revenge fantasy got us through many a dark hour.

"How about electrocution? She always has one of us draw her bath. We could throw in her hair dryer."

"Might work," Susan agreed.

It didn't. Turned out the wattage wasn't high enough. Of course, this was long before I started a course of self-improvement.

A loud moan woke me from my day nightmare. Daniel was trying to get my attention. He was thirsty and hungry and here I was standing around like a ninny.

CHAPTER 7
KATIE

MONDAY 12:09 P.M.

The Costco parking lot on McGillivray Boulevard was a hive of activity when I parked alongside the chain-link fence, one of the few spots left, meaning a long hike back to the grocery store under the unforgiving noonday sun. I grabbed my reusable bags and opened the driver's door, only to be greeted by a fiery blast furnace. The sweltering heat instantly turned my hair to frizz and my underarms to damp pools of sticky sweat. *Please don't let me run into anyone I know.*

I hadn't done any grocery shopping in weeks beyond the basics. In spite of the discomfort, I was looking forward to preparing dinner for my best friend, while hoping I could lure Ashley over for another try in helping her see reason.

The rush of cold air when the electronic door opened allowing me entry was a relief. I lined up and grabbed a cart alongside other sweaty customers that looked as enthusiastic as zombies. Pulling my members card from my wallet, I smiled at the greeter as I held it out for him to check. At his curt nod, I pushed my cart inside the big box store and took up my mental list of essential items.

In short order, I had half-filled my cart, incapable of turning down the deals, though I'm mostly buying for one. At the desert aisle, I dithered over a giant straw-berry cheesecake or triple chocolate brownies, finally settling on both. Sadie had a sweet tooth I wanted to encourage. She was far too thin, which made Ashley come to mind, and her slenderness. Did either of those women bother eating?

"Still enjoy sweets, I see." The voice I knew all too well made me look up from setting the tray of fancy desserts in my cart, careful to not squish the triple pack of rye bread. *Damn it, why now?* Seeing my ex always gave me heart palpitations and I avoided it whenever possible.

I coughed, clearing my throat, not daring to look Brad in the eyes but staring at a distant point over his left shoulder. "Yeah, well, having company so it seems appropriate."

"I'm Willow Sullivan by the way. Nice to meet you." A beautiful young woman grinned at me, showing far too many perfect teeth. *Yeah, I recognize you, always in the Winnipeg Free Press in the society section attending some charity function.* She was the only daughter of one of Winnipeg's big monied families. Figured. It was a toss-up which Brad loved more, money or prestige.

At least Brad was showing progress. First polite one in the string, bothering to introduce herself.

"Katie Kelly. Nice to meet you too." There, I deserved a reward for that whopper. I eyed a lovely Boston cream pie nearby, my fingers itching to pick it up, imagining it squashed all over the two faces hovering too damn close, its chocolate and yellow cream filling dripping off. Well, maybe only the one face. Instead, I dropped the third offering into my cart. *Let them make of that what they will.*

Insane. I'd be throwing it out or gaining more weight, either a poor option.

"You definitely got the right house for a party. River view, lots of room to entertain, unlike my condo with its lack of a backyard and nosey neighbors." Brad's dig at my keeping the house that had been bought with my money turned the snakes in my stomach to vipers.

"You got the lake house as well," I reminded him. "Too bad Riverbend's now filled with fake artwork thanks to you." I slam dunked my retort.

How is it my hands are now filled with a huge whipped cream and pumpkin pie? And then suddenly, most of it was smeared all over Brad's face, leaving only his greedy brown eyes visible.

I stepped back in horror and disgust and dropped the empty plate. The pumpkin filling did indeed look like baby poop. A froth of whipped cream surrounded my masterpiece, stuck in his perfect-styled hair and trendy beard.

"Oh my gosh!" Willow covered her mouth with one hand.

"What the hell, Katie!" Brad slopped most of the mess off his face with his hands, then stared at his fingers in disbelief. The floor surrounding us had become a road hazard. Too easy to slip on the ruined pie. Someone better alert the cleaning staff ASAP.

Other shoppers were stopping and staring now, some mouths having dropped open. Canadians were known for politeness, this event was so over the top that people had pulled out their cell phones, capturing the brouhaha for prosperity. Most excitement in a in a decade in a Costco, I'd bet.

"That's for taking my beloved dog, for making me sell the Warhol, and for all the women who have been cheated on in their lifetimes," I said through gritted teeth. I gathered what was left of my dignity and rushed to the front of the store, the only way to exit as a customer. I couldn't believe I'd done it. So many times I'd fantasied, of course, but I never thought I'd actually do it. Now I'd have to find another grocery store and time was slipping away. And a liquor store. No way was I getting through this hellish heat without a Tequila Sunrise or three waiting in the wings.

I managed to get into my vehicle before a series of three knocks on my side window made me startle. A woman stood there; her face wreathed in a grin. She gestured for me to lower the window with a hand bespeckled with large rings.

I did as she wanted. She looked harmless enough, her perspiring face and auburn curls surrounded by a massive straw sun hat. She was chewing gum and snapped it before speaking.

"I had to tell you well done! Wish I could have done that to my cheating ex."

I snorted. "Not my finest hour. I'll be lucky if they don't call the cops. Not to mention barring me from this store. I'm sure it was all captured in living color on CCTV."

She held up her phone. "I don't think they'd have the nerve. This might be the start of something. *#Women-throwing-pie-at-cheating-exes-in-grocery-stores*."

"Oh please no. I'm not one for being in the limelight," I groaned.

"Too late now, hon. Sometimes one has to step up and take it on the chin. Though I think you hit him more mid-face, judging by the mess." The woman laughed at her own wit followed by a choking sound as she began to cough.

"You okay?" Worried, I was about to disembark and perform the Heimlich maneuver. Was the gum caught in her throat?

She waved me off. "Fine, sure. Just a little tickle. You have a nice day now. I know I will."

She scampered away with a final cheerful wave, her flip-flops making a soft whooshing noise as her toes sunk deep into the leather. I groaned. Now it would be all over the internet. Nothing escaped scrutiny these days. *What have I done?*

I pounded the steering wheel with my fists, my eyes closed tight. Last thing I needed or wanted was untoward attention, which is why I had managed to keep myself strung together with therapy and vodka all these months. Stuck with no way to rewind the clock and undo the damage.

Things were getting away from me. Piling up. First forgetting the anniversary date. Then letting Ashley's situation dictate things. Now playing host to a juvenile revenge scenario that would only make things worse in the long run. I'd lost my grip, my perspective. *I should call Doctor Holt right now, make an emergency appointment.*

I turned on the radio to help drone out the images in my head.

"Authorities are once again dragging the Red River in hopes of finding the body of a young woman that went missing last week during the Red River Exhibition..."

My brain went into tilt mode. Dragging the river? What if they found something? This was bad. I had to warn Sadie.

I finished listening to the newscast that gave no more details only to look up and see a young couple pointing a finger at me from across the parking lot, one raising their fist in the symbol for universal triumph. Time to get the heck out of here and find a quiet store to shop in. Winnipeg maybe the biggest city in Manitoba, but it's never escaped its small-town roots. And in that moment, I could feel those roots surrounding me, strangling me, and trying to bring me down.

CHAPTER 8
ASHLEY

MONDAY 3:45 P.M.

"Where is she? She's been gone for hours. Damn it! What if she's decided to take a few vacation days? What will that do to the plan?"

"Then I'll have to check on *her* plans later at dinner."

The look on Quinton's face was priceless as my words sunk in. I kept my own expression on lock down.

"She invited *you* to dinner? Not us?"

"Sorry. She called a girl's night. No men allowed. No exceptions." Actually, I was looking to get away from this stifling place for a few hours, even if it was with the busy body across the street. The air was too thick with testosterone, sweat, and beer since Quinton was keeping all the doors and windows closed and locked to keep away prying eyes.

His eyes narrowed. "You're not thinking of pulling something?"

Men can be so stupid. I winced, remembering I'm supposed to be learning how to be a better human being, not be guilty of judging others. *Fake it till you make it, right?*

"What are you talking about? This can work to our advantage, Top Dog. I can gain her confidence before we set the ball rolling." It was a long shot, but maybe he'd fall for it.

He frowned, then turned back to watch the street again. His mind moved slowly, until it didn't.

"She's home."

"Good." I took an easier breath. "I'll get changed."

I headed for our bedroom and surveyed the slim choices in my old backpack I couldn't take a chance on unloading. The art of the con makes it necessary for one to be able to move at a moment's notice.

An image of my new neighbor rose in my mind, reminding me of how Katie dressed so nice, while my clothes came from Goodwill. Bet she never had to worry about choosing between something decent to wear and eating a meal. My life was in the dumper because of people like her who had it all. Envy rose, fueled by frustration, as I pulled out my few slim choices. She even owned a Warhol.

Stay focused. Never give the game away. Advice learned growing up in foster care. A tear slipped out as I pulled out the one wrinkled dress I owned that looked nice on me. And had the necessary pockets. Quinton had dropped a cigarette on it last time I wore it, leaving a small hole that spoiled the white background with the pink rosebud pattern. It would have to do. It was already hot as Hades today and nothing else was as loose or comfortable. But at least I could iron it, maybe find a needle and thread, and make myself look halfway presentable.

"What are you all gussied up for?" Quinton blew out a

puff of smoke in my direction, tainting the air with his underlying mistrust issues. "I thought it was just going to be a bunch of women?"

"It is. Well, just three of us. A friend of Katie's; Sadie, I think." I finished fixing the burned hole in the fabric the way I'd been shown, working the thread back and forth and creating a simple darning mesh to fill the hole. I cut the loose threads free and inspected my handiwork. Not too shabby. Only thing better would be a few sew-on appliqués.

"When did you get so domestic?" he sneered, coming closer into the laundry room where I'd located everything I needed to iron and fix clothes.

Defensive much. "Foster care has it uses. One of the families had a live-in grandma who could sew. She taught me a few tricks."

"Tricks, eh?" He ran his fingers up and down my arm, his expression shifting.

I winced, freezing in place. *Not now.* I needed a shower and I wanted to apply some makeup. Maybe put on a coat of nail polish. A part of me was darn sick of always looking like an unmade bed. The stink of Quinton's beer breath looming over me had me breathing shallowly through my nose.

A loud noise erupted of something crashing to the ground halted Quinton's hand. He turned his head to listen, his ferret eyes narrowing further.

"Did you check he was still secure when you went down to the basement?" he accused.

I nodded, my stomach roiling with unease. "What if he's broken lose?"

"Stay here."

Too antsy to stand still, I waited until he was out of

sight, then crept down the hallway after him to the top of the basement stairs.

"What the fuck do you think you're doing?" he shouted. Then the hard thuds of fists on soft flesh made me grimace. I had to stop this. Quinton's lack of control when he became riled was legendary. He'd kill Daniel if I didn't intervene. The homeowner didn't deserve to die, not like others I could mention.

I braced myself, then forced myself to descend the staircase, one step at a time, like a prisoner headed to the gallows. *Crap.* Quinton had Daniel in a choke hold around his neck. An image of being hung up by my own neck started me to shaking. My whole mind focused on an event that could never be erased until I was six feet under. *Stop. She was only fucking with you. You're here, right, she didn't manage to kill your spirit. Or your body. Let it go, Ashley.* I squeezed my eyes tight, both my hands hanging on tight to the banister like a lifeline.

Bitter bile filled the back of my throat and I wanted to spit it out. *Bad girl.* Reeling from the shock of the memory threatening my insanity, I no longer stood in Daniel's house, but in the attic of an old ramshackle house that should have been torn down years before. *"If you tell, I will kill you, hear me, bitch?" How could I not. He was yelling in my ear as he cut through the thick rope hanging down from the rafters and looped around my neck. My body slumped into his arms and it was all I could do not to throw up. My throat hurt so bad I wasn't sure I would ever be able to talk again.*

I missed a week of school, time enough to allow the bruises to fade and the pain to diminish. My one solace was reading, not something I ever shared. But somehow, they always figured it out and took them away for any perceived need to punish me. But that time had been different, books had been offered to keep me quiet.

"Get the fuck out of here!" Quinton screamed at me when he caught sight of me hovering on the stairs, bringing me lurching back to the present with a sickening wrench. His face contorted by rage, there was nothing left of the charismatic man I had been attracted to. Nothing but a murderous shell.

I wanted to run. I started to scramble back up the stairs, praying he wouldn't kill Daniel but the thought of going down as an accessory to murder stopped me in my tracks. I had to intervene, no matter the cost.

CHAPTER 9
KATIE

MONDAY 4:33 P.M.

I unloaded the hard-won groceries from the back seat of the Tesla and got right down to food prep. Halfway through assembling the marinade for the salmon fillets, I remembered. *Call Doctor Holt.*

Right. Maybe she could see me this week? I snorted. One way to make sure of it. Offload the video of my finest hour in Costco and send it to her. I was certain there'd be at least three versions available by now on social media, catching all the lovely different views and angles of the rousing altercation.

I picked up my iced Tequila Sunrise and took a big slug of the refreshing drink for courage. Then hiccuped as my esophagus spasmed from the extreme cold and hit of alcohol. *God, I'm such an idiot.*

Okay, no putting it off any longer. I punched in Dr. Holt's number and two rings later her receptionist answered.

"How may I help you?"

"I need an appointment soon as you can manage. This week—if possible. It's Katie Kelly calling."

A short silence. "Right. Can you come in this evening? The doctor will stay for you."

Her tone had changed meaning she knew the score.

"Sorry, I can't, I've got company coming, but tomorrow I'm free all day."

"Dr. Holt has an opening at seven a.m. Can you make that time?"

"Yes, thank you." I disconnected the call.

Seven a.m. was the signal for the good doctor wanting me off the damn streets ASAP. Well, in my opinion. But I did know firsthand, she didn't enjoy an early appointment having shared once in a moment of human weakness that mornings weren't her thing. *Don't be so worried sounding.* I sent the receptionist a positive mind message. It's not like I lobbed a live grenade at the guy for heaven's sake, just a pie loaded with whipped cream. The alcohol must have hit my system after a couple of days of scant eating, and I discovered, to my horror, I suddenly couldn't stop laughing. The look on Brad's prissy face. Priceless.

Tears streaming down my cheeks, I registered the doorbell ringing. Wiping my eyes with a tissue, I straightened my shoulders, took a deep breath, and hurried to answer.

But instead of seeing Sadie on the front step, there stood Ashley, two hours earlier than I had texted.

She looked shy, posing in a pretty print dress dotted with pink rosebuds and pasted smile, holding out an offering of a six-pack of beer. Minus one.

"I hope it's okay. It's all we had in the house. I thought maybe I could help you set up?" she asked, a nervous twinge in her voice. Right before she spoke, a millisecond of time, she had looked like a different person, one that raised the hackles on my neck. Like a wild animal in a cage, angry and mean. Then it vanished so quickly I wasn't certain I hadn't imagined it. A second later all I could see was a pathetic young girl needing a friend. Plus, she had a right to be angry, living in an abusive relationship. More a surprise it didn't boil over more, cause her to strike back. Of course, Quinton Riley was three times her size and looked like he lifted weights for a living, which would make anyone think twice about crossing him.

"Sure, no worries. Come in." I hid my annoyance that I wasn't ready to see her under a wider smile. Sometimes you're up to bat before you're ready and you'd best suck it up, think on your feet, not worry so damn much. But the self-message did nothing for the nerves firing off in my stomach again. Maybe I was picking up her vibes? She seemed nervous as hell, shaky under the plastered-on smile.

Ashley trailed me down the hall to the kitchen and when I glanced back at her I noted her checking out my furnishings and paintings again like she wanted to catalog everything for an appraiser.

"You sure do have a lot of beautiful things," she said. I noted the strain in her tone and wondered again about her life.

"You go to college, Ashley?"

She shook her head. "No, never got the chance. I left school in my final year. What can I do to help?" Just like my sister Rose, which didn't speak well for her future. She'd need to get her GED and get more training if she wanted a better life. And who doesn't want that? Maybe I could encourage her in some way tonight, create the right entry point to suggest it. Without a doubt Sadie would back up my advice.

"You can wash the lettuce," I offered, opening a cupboard and pulling out a strainer for the sink.

"Sure. One of my specialties."

I gave her a curious look that she picked up on.

"Cleaning. I tend to do a lot of it when I'm nervous or upset. Seems to be happening more all the time."

I ignored her innuendo. Maybe she wasn't aware of it, the sense of unease she gave off, like someone or something bad was stalking her? I didn't want her running off again. Best to build a rapport with her first, help make her receptive to listen to advice from a complete stranger.

"I like to pull weeds when I need time to calm down. Crochet or go for a run."

She grimaced, efficiently separating the lettuce leaves and rinsing them under the tap. "I've seen you out running, but it's not for me. I'm more a stay in and read kind of gal. And I have no idea how to crochet, though it does sound rather cool. Isn't that how you create fabric for things like throws or sweaters?"

"Yes, exactly like that. I'm right now making an afghan for my sister Rose for Christmas. What do you like to read?" I asked, pulling out a chopping board to cut up the vegetables for the salad.

"That's nice, making something for someone else. I read just about anything. I do love true crime best, though. Especially ones about women helping women. Like say a woman in a bad situation that needs help and a friend goes to bat for her, doing things she would not normally do but does it because it's a friend's life at stake. Maybe even something criminal, you know? I get that." She shook the water from the strainer. "What about you? What kind of stories do you like?"

I stopped mid-action of cutting the tomato into pieces. Was this only a freaking coincidence? Her scenario was too eerily similar to mine and Sadie's for comfort. But it had to be, I didn't know Ashley.

I found my voice and answered honestly. "I prefer fiction. Romances mainly." At least some couples had their fairy tale turn out, even if it was between the pages of a book.

Ashley wrinkled her nose. "Romances are definitely *not* my thing."

"You don't believe in true love?"

"No." She didn't elaborate but pursed her lips, like she was thinking about something that didn't bear mentioning.

I would have thought she'd believe in real love. That she was altruistic like so many young girls who had bad instincts about men. Wouldn't that make more sense, being with the ultimate bad guy, believing she could change him with enough outpouring of love and attention? Or maybe she did think that once upon a time but was slowly coming to the realization it would never exist with the likes of a Quinton Riley. She was not wrong if indeed that was where her thoughts were leading her. How I wished I could get inside her mind, help her find her true path, one that would give her the best life she could have. All my sisters deserved that.

"I did, believe that once," Ashley amended her statement as she caught sight of my surprised expression. "That I could change a person for the better."

"People can only change when *they* decide to. No outside pressure can make them change otherwise."

"You sound like you've been there. You know, tried to help someone?" she prompted.

I shrugged, running the celery under the tap, and breaking it apart with my fingers to get rid of the soil between the stalks. "I've only done what anyone would do if faced with a difficult situation. Helped a friend when it was necessary."

"How far does that go?" Ashley asked, sliding up closer to me, the knife still in her hand. The small gap between us made me uncomfortable and I leaned away. Then felt guilty. The poor girl was only after information, another perspective.

"Well, offer a safe haven when necessary. Things like that." I kept my expression nonchalant, not wanting to scare her off again.

"I get it. But what would you do if push came to shove?"

I was saved from answering, perhaps saying the wrong thing, by the ringing of the doorbell.

"I'll go," Ashley said.

"Better put the knife down first," I teased, deciding in the moment to give her the autonomy of going to answer the doorbell, fairly certain it was Sadie on the other side. My best friend would handle it well, I had no doubt, making the young girl feel right at home. Probably do a better job than I was managing.

"Yeah, right." She set the sharp blade aside and scurried from the room.

Without Ashley in the room, I felt a bit calmer, the stress rolling off my shoulders and uncrimping the tendons in my neck. Then I chastised myself. The poor girl was going through something she needed help with. I had my life figured out, for the most part. Even if today I had made a stupid choice to go after my ex. Not that I remembered it being a choice, more like a reaction I had not been expecting. Maybe I didn't have it figured out as well as I thought, blacking out and doing something so unexpected?

I could hear muffled voices getting closer and I turned around to greet my guests. Sadie's limp was more pronounced than usual and the memory of what had caused the problem for her hit me front and center. The memory of the knife's sharp blade slicing through the air, cutting into the back of her ankle threw me for a loop. Beads of sweat broke out over my skin as I took a deep breath to ground myself, then forced a smile of welcome.

"You two introduce yourselves?" I said, clearing my throat.

"Yes. I've brought vodka coolers," Sadie said with an affirmative nod to my question, holding out a carton of a dozen bottles of various flavors. Ashley followed right behind her, looking pleased.

"Thanks. Are we expecting a late night?" I asked. Sadie looked better than earlier, her expression more relaxed, her eyes clearer. She limped over to the counter and put the drinks down. Guilt at forgetting what day it was crept back and I pushed it aside. Now was not the time for self-pity.

"I got nowhere I have to be. I figured I've earned a short reprieve."

I grabbed a couple of tall glasses from the cupboard and added ice, handing them over to the two women. "Have at it. I've got all the fixings for Tequila Sunrises too. We can have a nice relaxing girl's night. Maybe play a game or watch a movie?" I suggested.

"Or throw a pie at an ex," Sadie said with a wide grin as she poured a cooler into one of the glasses.

"Oh, shoot. You saw the video." My heart stuttered as my body remembered all too vividly fleeing from the store. A moment of shame captured for eternity.

"What the heck, girl, you're famous! Wish I'd thought of that."

"What are you talking about?" Ashley asked, her expression intrigued.

Sadie took out her phone, fingers flying over the screen. "Take a gander at this," she said, sharing the video with Ashley.

The young girl put her hand over her mouth, her eyes widening. "Oh, my goodness!"

"It was stupid, okay. I didn't realize I had done anything until it was too late."

"Not sure that defense will hold up in court," Ashley said with an unfathomable look. It made me more uncomfortable.

"Darn it, civil court. Do you think he'll sue me? Or set the cops on my ass?"

Sadie shook her head, giving Ashley a small frown. "I doubt it. He was the one that cheated, not you. Brad's the one who looks bad. Plus, you got an army of women at your back. Look at the string of positive comments."

I glanced at her phone, relieved to see that what she was reporting was true. No exaggeration, my moment of insanity was playing well to home field advantage.

"Guess I'm not the only one."

"A toast to the newest social internet star," Sadie said, clinking her glass with mine and then Ashley's. "Maybe this will start a new trend. Pies in the face of cheating lovers. Sure beats burning clothes and possessions on the front lawn. The fire department will thank you, especially since we're in a drought this summer. I mean, have you seen a hotter summer in Winnipeg?" Sadie shook her head, downing half her fruit-flavored cooler in one long gulp.

"Okay, salad's already." I covered the bowl with plastic wrap and placed it in the fridge. "Shall we sit and have cocktails on the patio or in the living room? There's a lot of shade in the backyard and I have personal fans at the ready."

"I vote for the patio," Sadie said, raising her eyebrows at Ashley.

Ashley nodded so I grabbed a bowl of salty snacks and directed us through the French doors into the backyard.

"This is so nice," Ashley said, glancing around and choosing a lawn chair set around the round patio table. "Perfect place to get rid of a body."

I blinked.

Sadie stared at me; her eyes wide open in shock.

"Oops, sorry, did that spill out." She placed a hand over her mouth in mock horror, then pulled it away to explain. "I was noticing how your property connects with the Red River and you must know about all the bodies being dumped in there these past years on the news."

I nodded, sickened by the earlier news cast I still hadn't shared with my friend and of the memory of the Red Dress women. A terrible situation. Vulnerable mostly Aboriginal women dead at the hands of their abusers. Here, and over at the Brady Landfill. Forensic investigations were ongoing, with land feasibility studies undertaken to decide how best to proceed.

"Horrendous crimes," Sadie said, her earlier happier mood evaporating right in front of my eyes. "Senseless." She reached down and rubbed the back of her leg. A thick ropey scar ran around the back of her heel, then branched upward a few inches to divide her calf muscle in two.

I took a slug of my drink, needing to drown out the images of the tiny red dresses representing each life. And of the image of who had caused my friend's pronounced scar.

"No woman should end up dead at the hands of a man," I said, my stomach twisting in knots.

"Or vice versa."

I looked over at Ashley in shock and dismay. She turned beet red but stood her ground. "Women do it sometimes too. Kill men."

Sadie shook her head. "Not nearly as much as men kill their partners."

"Well, just sayin'."

How had Asley's viewpoint gotten so distorted, that she thought you could compare the two? How much had Quinton Riley to do with it? Filling her mind with all sorts of twisted ideas. Certainly, there were female monsters, like Karla Homolka in Canada, and Aileen Wuornos in the states. Less than fifteen percent of serial killers were female. It was far more likely for a woman to be killed by a man than the other way around. Of course, neither was acceptable, both being the work of a psychopath.

But all this proved was Ashley needed counseling. Guidance. More than I realized. *First seek to understand, then to be understood.* The wise words of my grandmother, a better, kinder person than any I had met in this lifetime.

CHAPTER 10
ASHLEY

I picked up my drink and drained it. My words had gone over like a lead balloon. Socially awkward or what? I needed to fix my faux pas fast.

"How about I get us refills?" I suggested, jumping to my feet.

"Sure. I could use one," Sadie said, handing me her glass. Katie did likewise. No one got up to help which was fine. They probably wanted to talk about their weird guest behind my back.

I slipped in through the sliding door, left it partially open and placed the two glasses on the counter. My phone vibrated with an incoming text and I glanced at it. Quinton. I chewed on my non-existent thumbnail and considered the timing. Not yet. I ignored the message and grabbed a cooler from the fridge along with the orange juice for the Tequila Sunrise.

Placing the heavy-on-the-alcohol drinks on a tray in preparation for rejoining the two women while mine was alcohol free. When should I spring the good news on them? I wondered, rolling it over in my mind. Later, when they were both more inebriated would be more effective, I decided before I hurried down the hall toward the bathroom to relieve myself. The window was closed but I carefully opened it a couple of inches by cranking the handle, aware that it was right across from the patio table, preparing to eavesdrop.

"She needs our help, you know, more than she realizes."

I rolled my eyes at Katie's lame words, unable to hear Sadie's murmured reply. What I needed was money, not help or advice. The only way out of my situation was a big score. The Warhol in her living room was an answer to a prayer.

"Did you hear they are dragging the Red River looking for bodies again?" Katie said.

"No, that's not good," Sadie said it more loudly than she had been speaking before.

Interesting. I filed the information away and leaving the window open exited the bathroom.

My phone vibrated in my pocket again but I ignored it. I wanted some girl time, was that too much to ask?

"Here we go," I said, setting the tray on the tabletop and unloading the frosty drinks.

"Thanks," Katie said while Sadie gave a nod and picked up the glass.

"To new friends," Katie toasted, then took a sip.

"Not going to be in town long enough to make real friends, I'm afraid," I said with a sad little smile.

"Where do you hail from?" Sadie asked, peering at me over her glass.

I shrugged. "All over. Moved too many times to count. How about you?"

"We both moved to Winnipeg soon as we could.

Small-town friends," Katie answered for her, giving her a look that appeared to be one of warning. Why?

My antenna went up as things became clearer. Both from the same small town? Meant they most likely have known each other since they were children. Had a nice, long friendship. Something I longed for myself.

"How come you lived so many different places, Ashley? Were your family in the military?" Sadie asked.

I shook my head. "Nothing like that. I was in foster care since I was a baby. My mom gave me up, said she couldn't handle another kid. I think she was in an abusive relationship and wanted me to be safe. Thinking that helps me a lot." Didn't help at all on nights when I felt abandoned, unwanted, and uncared for, like I could disappear and no one would notice I was gone.

"I'm sorry. It must have been tough," Katie said, her expression empathetic.

"Yeah, well, it did teach me a lot about people. More than I would have liked at times. But some families were nice, you know." I shrugged, fiddling with my napkin. "You're always the new kid, meaning you can never be part of the family as it can all be taken away from you so quickly it can make your head spin if someone doesn't like you. Or accuses you of something."

"Did that happen a lot? Being moved on for something you may or may not have done?" Katie asked softly.

"When I was little, I got the benefit of the doubt, but later, when I started to change, grew breasts, and the men began to notice, it got harder. The moms wanted me gone."

"Have you had any therapy?" Sadie asked, her eyes darkened with some intense emotion.

I pretended to give her question some thought,

wanting to spin it my way. "Not really. Once you turn eighteen, you're thrown out of the system with very little help." I needed to redirect this conversation, uncomfortable with how much these two women were learning about my life. "What about you two, what town did you grow up in?"

I watched the pair exchange a look again, with Sadie giving the nod. How strange? Was their hometown some kind of mystery? *Something happen there?* My pulse quickened.

"We both grew up in Northern Manitoba, a little town called Casper, near God's River," Kate said, her mouth flattening into a thin line.

Shocked at the name, I tried desperately to hide my response from them, coughing into my hand for a moment before responding. "Judging from your expression, it looks like people weren't very nice to you there. Figures, lots of stuck-up people in this world. Thinking they're better than you because they have an expensive house and pots of money." I covered my mouth with my hand again. "Sorry, I didn't mean you. You're nice, well, duh, we only met and you're making me supper and all. Introduced me to your friend. But not so nice to exes, eh." I giggled, remembering the video of her throwing pie in his face. "I wish I had the courage. Though I think it's cool you got this great house in the divorce."

"Riverbend was mine before the marriage. Brad got the lake property and cash. He's a lawyer by trade and got help from a colleague for a better settlement than he deserved." Katie grimaced and took a large gulp of her drink before choking and taking a deep breath, her hand over her chest. "Wow, you make a stiff drink, Ashley. But I need to be clear, I shouldn't have done it, thrown the pie. It was the wrong thing to do. I don't know what came over me."

"A lot of women out there think what you did was good. I wouldn't worry about it. Besides, it would be worth getting a restraining order or sued or whatever it is people do who are targeted." I meant to reassure her, but instead Katie looked more worried than before.

"No one's suing anyone. Come on, drink up," Sadie said, downing her glass of well spiked strawberry cooler.

"What do you do for a living, Sadie?" I asked, sipping my bright blue soft drink I'd found in Katie's fridge. I liked the color and the blueberry taste.

"I work from home, same as Katie." Sadie seemed uncomfortable with the question, accordioning her napkin over and over and not looking me in the eye. My life had well prepared me for knowing when someone is lying. It could be the difference between being left alone and being hit. So when I spotted one, I filed it away, careful to not strike a hornet's nest. But this was a common everyday question. So why lie about her occupation?

"You create apps too?" I pressed. "That sure pays well I imagine. If I ever get to go to college, I think computer programming would be the golden ticket." Then I gave it more thought, remembering the inexpensive and well-used vehicle Sadie had driven up in and parked in the driveway. "But you're not as successful as Katie, right? Still waiting for your big payday?" I knew I was talking too much, but I truly wanted to see how these two women ticked, why they were such good friends. Seemed a great opportunity to learn more about something I sucked at.

"Katie has a far better head for business than I do."

The announcement didn't seem to bother either woman and Katie was quick to defend her friend.

"Sadie's better with real people. I'm best at machine language. Long hours, and living like a hermit doesn't bother me. And likely after today's episode, I'll need to start having my groceries delivered too."

I decided to stay away from the touchy subject, for now. "You got loads of friends then, Sadie. I envy you. That's so nice, to have friends you can count on when the chips are down."

Sadie twisted her lips to one side, a tell she was uncomfortable. "Not so many. I just like to keep the ones I do have. Be there for them, like Katie has been there for me over the years. More than I deserve."

"You guys are so-o lucky. What I wouldn't give for a friend who stood by me no matter what." I gave a long dramatic sigh. "You know like they always say, help you bury the body."

"We should stay in touch after you move on," Katie said, leaning in and looking quite animated by the idea. She ignored my suggestion about burying bodies.

"I'd like that." I reached out and patted her hand, difficult as it was for me to touch another human being. I swallowed hard when she grasped my fingers in hers and gave them a squeeze, not letting go. Distaste soured my stomach and I fought the bile rising in my throat. After a decent interval I tugged my hand away, hoping she wouldn't be offended by my actions.

My phone vibrated again and I glanced at it, grimacing. "Oh Lord, I gotta go. Quinton's on the warpath."

CHAPTER 11
KATIE

MONDAY 5:41 P.M.

A terrible sense of unease struck with Ashley's announcement, sending chills racing down my spine in spite of the languid heat. "You know you don't have to go back there, right? You can stay here."

Ashley gave a head bob, her eyes dark and troubled, though she pretended otherwise. "No worries. He's missing his beer. Since no one is drinking it anyway, I'll take it to him. That's if no one wants one? Not like I'm drinking alcohol anyway."

Sadie and I shook our heads to the negative. Then I picked up on her last comment.

"What? You're not drinking with us? Why not, Ashley?" A sense of foreboding destroyed what good feeling I'd built up over having Sadie visit and introducing her to Ashley. *What if what I suspect is true? Is she pregnant? Please, please just let it be an aversion to alcohol.*

But she patted her tummy to my horror. Oh no, this screamed disaster. I tried to hide my misgivings with a small smile, but when the young girl looked at me, she appeared confused by my lack of enthusiasm and I knew I'd not been able to hide my anxiety.

"Yes, we're expecting. The baby's due in six months." She looked a bit lost, like she'd been expecting congratulations, not to have two women staring at her in total disbelief. Sadie was silent by my side and I realized I had to step up, say something. Cover up the faux pas.

"Wow, you caught me off-guard. I guess congratulations are in order. How's the father taking it?"

"Quinton's fine about it." She shrugged and chewed at her non-existent fingernails. "Once he sees the baby he'll be overjoyed, you wait and see. I'll be back in a jiff." Ashley leaped to her feet, scurrying away before I could say anything else.

"That girl is in deep trouble," I announced before turning on my personal fan, the heat of anger at the man across the street thinking he could interrupt with such a lame demand made breathing harder, like I was suffocating underground. The thought of her being pregnant had raised the stakes so much I couldn't discuss it yet. I'd either break into tears or start throwing things.

"She seems to know how to handle him," Sadie said.

"What? She has no idea how this thing could play out." I hated to disagree with my best friend, but it was like Ashley's plight was not concerning her at all. Had she forgotten what it was like to be in an abusive relationship? I found it impossible to believe, meaning something else must be distracting her. Maybe finding out Ashley was pregnant was causing her too much emotional turmoil for her to think straight? That had to be it, Sadie was nothing if not sympathetic.

"I hate to say this, but she's up to something. I can feel it. Something's not quite right here, Katie." Sadie looked away as she said it, her expression speculative. So that was it.

"What on earth could she be up to? She's a young girl in an abusive relationship. You, of all people, should understand that."

Sadie paled, and guilt pressed down on me. Hard. She had obviously also picked up on Ashley's strangeness, her odd answers. I chalked it up to how twisted her life had been, growing up in foster care and all that had happened to her since, but Sadie seemed to read something far more sinister in her responses.

"Sorry. You're right. She's a little off. But I think we need to give her a pass. She's had it rough and now another life is involved." I leaned in toward Sadie, as if I could somehow help her see what I did.

"You're right. I'll try to keep an open mind." My friend took my words on the chin, seeming to come right around. I admired that ability in her. But maybe that was why it had taken her so long to see Wyatt for what he was? Horrible to think such a good quality as being able to see another side of the issue was what had caused her such incredible pain and loss in her life. She had always given him the benefit of the doubt, given second and third chances, and look what it led to. Maybe I was wrong in asking this of her, wanting her help with Ashley? Especially considering how my aiding her all those years ago had led to the worst disaster possible considering the situation. The past came creeping back in all its horrific detail as if it had happened only yesterday, breeching all the walls of my defensive strategy I'd spent considerable time shoring up over the years, probably because I was now faced with Ashley's escalating situation.

That last couple of days had been the worst of all. It had led to a future that had changed beyond recognition, that could never be undone. It had started out quiet enough and I was preparing to head off to college in another week. Alone. The summer had flown by though. First Sadie and Wyatt's small wedding with the bride six months pregnant. Me helping her to move into the rented trailer to await the birth of their baby, even begging my mother for anything she didn't need to help give my best friend a decent start.

Then Sadie had called me. Frantic. Wyatt had gone crazy. He'd been drinking all day, saying how he was too young to be saddled with a cheating wife and kid. Was it even his? That she should have had an abortion like he wanted her to. She was frightened, locked in the bathroom. Could I come over? She wanted to leave but she was afraid to try by herself. He might hurt the baby. She didn't want to call the cops on him; he was already in a heap of trouble, having had an altercation in the local bar earlier in the week. With the baby due in only a matter of few weeks, she was certain he'd straighten up once it came. She was so certain that it would be all it would take. See its beautiful face and he'd fall straight in love. Be the man he'd promised to be.

I didn't believe a word of it. Sadie was delusional. Wyatt was on his way to becoming a full out abuser. Today was only proving me right. We argued. But I said I was on my way. I wanted to call another friend, sensing having some back up would be a good idea. She begged me not to. Said she was embarrassed enough as it was. She didn't need anyone else seeing the bed she'd made for herself. She was so upset by the idea I promised to go alone. A mistake that would haunt me forever.

"Are you okay?" Sadie was looking at me like she had been trying to get my attention for a while.

I sat up and cleared my dry throat. "I'm fine."

"You looked like you zoned out there for a moment.

So, what's the plan? Anything I can do to help get Ashley off to a better place?" Sadie asked before taking a sip of her drink, her eyes troubled.

I hesitated to share more, but the passage of things beyond my control was pressing down on me. "I wish we had more time, but they're only here for a few days. I don't know, maybe sharing a bit of your personal experience might help?" It was a lot to ask and I wouldn't be surprised if she turned me down flat. But maybe it would be good for her to talk about it with someone other than me?

Sadie leaned back in her chair, as if trying to get away from it or away from me. Then she shook her head, her expression distant. "I don't think I can do that. Revisit my life with a stranger. There's got to be another way to convince her to get help."

"Forget I asked. It's too much, I get it."

"How about we talk about bad boyfriends or husbands in general? Site a few celebrity cases? Get her to see parallels between them and the way this Quinton guy treats her. Or maybe get her talking more? Build some trust."

I believed trust and rapport was easier to build when one laid bare the hard facts of their own life, but that was off the table.

"I hope she comes back tonight." What was going on right now in Daniel's home? Was Ashley in trouble for coming over here? Would it be hard for her to get away again? All sorts of worrisome scenarios began to build in my mind, my knees jiggling under the table.

The doorbell rang and I sprung up to answer it. But it wasn't Ashley on the other side, but my ex with a disgruntled expression that did not bode well. And after what had happened earlier today, I knew I had it coming.

CHAPTER 12
ASHLEY

"Here's your beer. Are we good now?" I plunked the beer down on the living room coffee table, suspecting Quinton was already half soused. He leaned back on the sofa, his legs sprawled, his hair an untidy mess and reeking of alcohol. "You're the one on duty tonight. Are you going to be able to say awake?" The first slurred words out of his mouth confirmed it.

"You...you need to re...reread the list again. You're beginning to slip, Ashley. Where's the smile...I'm entitled to?"

"I don't have time for this." I tapped my foot on the hardwood floor, wanting desperately to get the hell out of there. We'd had one mishap earlier, one that could have ended badly if the guy in the basement had managed to get any further. As it was, he'd done a bang-up job of destroying the pipe he was connected to, meaning the basement smelled of the sewer. Plus the refrigerator had been knocked over, the bang we'd heard. Quinton had gone into a rage, popping the guy a few times before making sure that wouldn't happen again and would most likely have strangled him to death if I hadn't intervened. This time he'd taken the time to drill into the cement wall and attached a secure hook. Daniel's hands were now secured behind his back, an uncomfortable position. Something I had firsthand knowledge of.

His expression turned ugly. "You don't have time! Don't you forget my part in all this. Hell, if it wasn't for me, you'd still be laying down for punters on Higgins and Main."

"I *never* did that!" My heart rate jacked up at the disgusting reference. Why did he always have to ruin everything? Throw jobs of muck on others. Was his ego that frigging fragile?

I needed to appeal to his greed. "We agreed to leave all that in the past. We gotta stay smart, focus on this score. You know it will set us up for a long time."

"Fine. But don't forget who you're dancing with. No one makes a fool out of me. Not even you." He stabbed a finger in my direction, his eyes hooded and dark.

Why would they when you're so good at doing that for yourself.

"I'm just saying we need to concentrate, get this job done first."

"Yeah, whatever." He punctuated his dissing remark with a belch, opening a fresh beer. I held my tongue on asking how many that was. He knew as much as I did that we needed to keep our heads tonight.

I moved away and peeked out the living room window. Shoot. An SUV was parked in the driveway now. What did they want? A man and a woman had gotten out, tugging a collie dog on a leash. The man picked it up and held it in his arms while pushing the doorbell. I didn't like the look of this. Maybe they'd be staying for a while? Last thing I needed was a pair of do-gooders getting in our way.

"She's got company," I said, not taking my eyes off them. "Looks like the woman is filming it. They look familiar. Damn, it's the pair from the video. Her ex and his new squeeze. They're up to something."

Curiosity must have gotten the best of Quinton because he joined me at the window. "Looks like he's handing her the dog. Weird."

"I'd guess to make up for how shitty he looks online. It went viral, *#revenge-on-cheating-exes*. She threw a pie at him earlier today in the grocery store. Screaming about his cheating on her and making him look a fool." I'd enjoyed it more than I admitted.

"Really, what a bitch."

"She had provocation," I said without thinking. "The guy was cheating on her."

Quinton stilled at my side. "Time for a correction, Ashley?"

CHAPTER 13
KATIE

MONDAY 6:12 P.M.

"What do you want, Brad?" I asked, holding my arms crossed tight against my chest, not looking at him. The memory of earlier still burned and there was no doubt this visit was going to be part of my comeuppance. I closed my eyes, waiting, expecting a pie in the face or some other such punishment for earlier. Not like I didn't deserve it. I groaned, disappointed in my lack of maturity. Was I ever going to grow up? Why hadn't I walked away? Left the vicinity and kept my dignity. Instead, I had let the past year of escalating interactions with him to finally come to this. A pie throwing event in a food store for all the world to witness. Unbelievable. And beyond stupid.

"Open your eyes, Katie. I've come bearing gifts."

"Gifts?" The word was so at odds with anything remotely possible to do with my ex that I blinked then open without thinking. Took a better look. Was it possible?

Brad was standing there holding Andy in his arms. Willow stood back a bit and off to the side, holding her phone up obviously recording our interactions.

"I've brought you Andy. Here," he said, plunking him in my arms like he was a suitcase. "I realized after what happened today that you need him more than me. Andy is your emotional support animal and I want to see you get better, Katie. So Willow and I talked, and, voilà, here he is. Are you sure you up to looking after him? If not, we can take him home and bring him back for visits. Maybe that would be best? I know after what happened today that you're going through something bad." He held out his arms, looking like he was being the best guy in the world.

Passive aggressive much? He normally avoided all direct communication like the plague. Dumbfounded didn't have cover it as I stood there, incapable of uttering a single word. This was not like my ex at all. He never did anything out of the kindness of his heart. Everything was calculated, down to the nickel for even a tip left in a restaurant. I used to think it charming until it wasn't. But there was way more to this situation that I was too overwhelmed with emotion to question at the moment.

I pushed my face into Andy's silky fur, choking back a sob. I had missed him so much every single day. He began to lick my face, his tail wagging wildly.

"I can take care of him fine," I said firmly. No way was Andy going anywhere now. He'd made the offer, obviously now that I thought about it, to try to alleviate the damage from earlier on his part. But he was quali-fying it by suggesting I wasn't up to looking after Andy, hoping I'd back down and go with "visits." No way was he getting away with it. I could take care of my dog, while Brad was known for complaining about having to walk him twice a day. I'd bet my now fake Warhol on it that it was Willow who took care of most of Andy's daily needs. She was too good for Brad.

"Thank you," I said, too tense to smile.

I held on to Andy with both hands and hurried back inside, slamming the door behind me before Brad could wrench him from my arms like I could tell he wanted to. All Willow had to do was stop recording and the part where he rescinded his offer would not be seen by the world. Selective imaging. The way of the world now.

More loud knocking ensued on the door that I completely ignored. I reluctantly set Andy down to lock all three deadbolts. I wasn't taking chances now that a wrong had been corrected.

Wow. I was truly and completely stunned at this turn of events. Who could have known that my earlier misbehavior brought about after months of stress and torment could result in such a positive event. Andy was home. And in the moment, I forgave it all. Even having to sell my beloved Warhol. But try to take Andy back now, asshole, and expect the wrath of a woman scorned. I had the upper hand for once in my life and I wasn't letting it go. Not for Brad, not for anybody. Not when it came with having my beloved furry baby home. I would have thrown a thousand pies if I'd known this would be the end result. Been made a complete ridicule of to have Andy back.

"Let's get you settled," I said out loud. Then hummed a victory chorus of Queen's "We Are the Champions" all the way into the kitchen to check on supplies. The knocking continued but I blissfully ignored it. Possession is nine-tenths of the law, right? I wanted to enjoy this moment. Make it last. It was the best one in a very,

very long while. Truthfully, I couldn't remember the last time I felt this good.

I rummaged around inside Andy's cupboard that some would accuse me of keeping as a shrine to my favorite guy. It was filled with all his supplies and toys. I found his water bowl and feeding dishes before checking the dates on the dozen or so tinned dog food. Still viable. Good, because I didn't want to venture out yet. I wanted to stay holed up here, making sure no one could dognap Andy when I wasn't looking.

"Here we go, boy. Your favorite taster's choice dog food." I filled both dishes, one with water, and set them on his mat.

He barked his thanks once and set right in. He's always been a messy eater, hence the mat, but it was wonderful to see him wagging his tail, his ears perky. I could have sat on the floor and watched him for hours if not days. He was my calm in a storm, always able to bring me around from my worst funk.

"Wow, is that Andy?" Sadie asked. She'd just come in from outside through the patio doors, an empty glass in her hand.

"Sure is." I got to my feet, keeping an eye on him. "Brad needed to do something apparently because of all the feedback online. God bless the social internet is all I say, because tonight, it brought Andy home. Brad and Willow were going to rescind the offer, make it visits because, of course, I wasn't up to looking after him, but I didn't let that happen. I ducked right back inside and I'm staying put until they leave." I quickly walked over and locked the patio doors, then pulled the venetian drapes across the chain and twisted the cord to close them tight. I didn't want the pair suddenly inside my home, demanding Andy now that they had their proof of them being the nice guys already recorded for posterity.

"Good thinking," Sadie said. "Want me to check if they're gone? The knocking has stopped."

"Would you please? I just can't let him out of my sight yet. It's been so long." Tears filled my eyes. He had to take my dog and leave me all alone. When it happened, I'd checked online, trying to find out if others had been through the same ordeal. And yeah, it was fairly common. Everyone seemed to fight over who got the family pet in times of divorce. Losing access to their dog or cat was considered as or nearly as emotionally wrenching as losing their spouse. Like a one-two punch. A spike in cases involving family pet disputes had risen alarmingly since COVID, according to intel I'd gathered during my desperate search to find a way to keep Andy. But he'd been Brad's dog first, so the judge ruled in his favor. And I was left out in the cold to grieve.

"Well, that's all over now, eh, Andy. We can go running together again in the mornings, walk down by the river at nights, spend lots of time napping and reading."

Sadie came back into the room and headed for the booze area we'd set up on the counter. "They're still parked in the driveway. Probably uploading the video." She rolled her eyes as she refilled her glass with ice and liquor, topping it up with orange juice. "Clever though. But I think it backfired. Looks like this little guy is home to stay." She gave a head nod at my furry baby.

Andy looked over at her, wagging his tail with delight. "I think so too. He's not going anywhere. Once they upload that video, Andy's all mine. Home to stay. That will be proof positive they willingly gave him back to me."

Andy gave a quick bark of agreement. We'd always been simpatico, psychic even. On the same schedule, seeming to think alike. He wasn't into throwing pumpkin pie, though his nipping at my ex wouldn't have caused me any grief.

"Want another drink?" Sadie asked.

"Yes, I feel like celebrating now," I said, letting my guard down and allowing a sensation of pleasure flow through me. It was such a rare feeling, I wasn't certain it was real at first, but the twinges grew into a warmth that flared throughout my body. *Serenity now*. My mantra for all occasion. One I had conveniently forgotten earlier today. But karma, for once, was on my side. Nothing can ruin this day, I decided, I won't let it. If only I knew what was coming next, I would have kept my guard up, kept the universe from sending a harsh dose of reality to counterbalance the good thing that had just happened. *Why is the yin and yang so extreme at times? Like soon as you're happy, it has to throw a wrench into the mix?*

But blissful for the moment, Sadie and I sat down at the kitchen table, enjoying our drinks.

"Oops, I just realized. All the snacks are still on the picnic table. Want me to go get them?" she asked.

I waved her off. "Leave them. I'm not taking the chance at opening the door again tonight. They might be lurking out there, waiting to pounce. I've got lots of things on hand we can eat. I did a big shop today." Then I remembered I should have bought a large jug of water for my safe room. I liked to change it up every six months or so. I'd lugged the last one out into the hallway for exchanging for fresh, but today had been so shredded that I had missed taking the empty container back to the store for a refill. Something else I could blame on Quinton Riley.

"Good thinking." She took another sip of her drink. "Do you think she's coming back tonight?"

"Maybe, I don't know. If not, I'll check round tomorrow and see how she is."

"What if it's too late?" Sadie chewed at her bottom lip and then caught me staring at her, the look on my face obviously reflecting my worry as her words sunk in. "I'm sorry. I'm spoiling your party. I shouldn't have said it."

"No, that's not true." Though it was. Now I couldn't help but feel the anxiety flow back through me again, replacing my very short interlude of contentment. My stomach lining reacted, roiling with unease. "You're right. We can't leave it until tomorrow. I'll text, and if she doesn't answer within a few minutes, I'll head straight over there." I pulled out my phone as I spoke, firing off a few words to Ashley.

We waited.

I drilled my fingers on the tabletop, envisioning the worst. Why is it I do that? I needed to get a grip. She was most likely fine. He knew we were across the street, keeping an eye out for her. He'd made that clear earlier, something that displeased him to no end, me having any interactions with her. Actually, now that I thought about it, it was rather surprising she had come over at all. Surely he had thrown ice water at the idea? But yeah, like his displeasure was going to stop me from marching over there in a few more minutes if I didn't hear back from Ashley. She needed to be treated well, especially in her condition. Stress was bad for the baby. Any baby. Thoughts of Sadie's tiny baby girl, her delicate, translucent skin that had showed the blue veins underneath had me about ready to run screaming across the street, which would be of no help to anyone. I needed to keep

81

my wits about me. Stay focused. Logical. No matter how difficult.

I sent a second text, saying I was coming over if she didn't respond in the next two minutes.

"Okay." I stood up abruptly, not bothering to wait more than thirty seconds. Such a bad feeling had come over me that I envisioned Ashley's dead body waiting somewhere inside Daniel's home. "I'm going over there."

"I'm coming with you."

I nodded in agreement. "Thanks. I appreciate the support."

"No problem."

We marched out of the kitchen and through the living room together. Suddenly, a loud pounding erupted on the front door.

We both jumped, nerves strung out on a thin razor wire, tugging and vibrating between us.

"Let me in! Please! He's after me!"

"Oh my goodness! It's Ashley!" I half-shouted.

I slammed my way through, opening the three dead-locks, cursing at the delay, cursing at my need for them. But not in my wildest dreams had I expected to be letting someone in, the locks were there to keep the bad guys out.

CHAPTER 14
KATIE

MONDAY 7:13 P.M.

Finally I had unlocked all the deadbolts and was able to wrench the door open, perspiration beading on my skin. Ashley stood on the front step, tears streaming down her face, her body quaking. Observing no one else around, my heart in my throat with worry and anxiety, I tugged her inside the living room and slammed the door shut.

"Check that she's okay and not hurt, Sadie, will you?" I asked, incapable of doing anything else for the moment but reengaging the locks. Satisfied we were once again secure, I turned to check out the young girl. Sadie had taken the young girl into her arms, Ashley's sobs echoed loudly in the small space. My friend patted and rubbed circles on her back, trying her best to soothe her.

"It's fine now. You're safe with us," Sadie said, her tone motherly.

When Ashley calmed down enough, we led her to the sofa. I noted there was some slight bruising over one eye, but otherwise she seemed unscathed unless there were bruises I couldn't see.

Her story spilled out in dribs and drabs between gasps and the occasional sob. We remained silent for the most part, letting her tell her truth and only prompting her when she drifted off. We both knew the value of letting it out, both of us having both failed miserably to do that, keeping everything bottled up until it was too late. And look where it landed us. I should have demanded Sadie tell me everything, now feeling guilty of I'd thought she was dissing me when she clammed up or covered up the truth, saying how great everything was. *Pay attention to your gut feeling, it will tell you so much more than anything else if you let it.*

"And he's never done this before? Hit you and threatened to harm you?" I asked in complete disbelief at her continued denials that this was so out of the blue, saying it was so unlike Quinton, that it had never happened before. She quit shaking her head at my skeptical tone, not looking me in the eye. And how sad those blue eyes were, all red-rimmed and filled with anguish. How deep did this abuse go?

"How has long has it been going on?" I asked.

She shrugged. Then answered in a little girl voice. It tugged at something deep inside me. "A while. Since he found out about the baby. He thinks we're too young. That we're not ready, not prepared for the big changes a child will bring. And the problem is, he's right. We have no permanent address yet. Still housesitting or staying with friends. Sometimes we stay in shelters." She turned red at the confession, obviously filled with shame at her predicament.

"No shame in asking for help, Ashley," Sadie said. "I wish I had sooner."

"You? You've been abused?"

A loud pounding at the front door halted the conversation in its tracks. Quinton Riley had arrived.

"You got to hide me. Didn't you say something about having a safe room somewhere?" Ashley whimpered, looking around frantically, her eyes widened with terror. "Quinton won't give up until he breaks in."

The right thing to do would be to call the police. But I hesitated to mention this, not wanting to be on their radar, not with the secrets that existed between Sadie and me. My friend needed to stay safe as much as Ashley. I had promised her we would never reveal anything about our former lives together, no matter what the provocation. Us having to give our names over to the cops threatened exposure. But it seemed fate was testing us. Was it because we needed to reaffirm our commitment to each other or was it because we needed to think beyond ourselves?

"We can hide there until he either gives up or goes away." I ignored the startled look from Sadie that questioned my decision because I wasn't certain either if it was the right thing to do. What if he makes himself at home? Waits us out? But I could see nothing else for us to do. I jumped to my feet and tugged Ashley along behind me to my office off the living room. One bit of good luck, there was a camera system installed and we'd know some of what was going on.

Sadie hurried along behind us, having taken a moment to grab her purse.

"Get Andy, would you?" I yelled over my shoulder at her. I yanked open the door to the safe room, ushering Ashley inside. With the four of us it would be a tight squeeze, but we could manage. Surely he would give up when he couldn't find us in the house? The only way in was to break a window because I knew for a fact they were all locked tight. It stood to reason he might not want to do something that could alert another neighbor. I was guessing he needed time to calm down. And time in the safe room would give me ample time to talk Ashley into getting proper help, which was the silver lining because this time she couldn't deny it.

"Wait here," I said. I hurried out of the room, searching frantically for Sadie and Andy. I found them in the kitchen, Andy hiding under the table.

"Come here, boy," Sadie said, trying to coax him out. I could hear the worry underlining her tone.

"Andy, come to mama." I joined her in trying to coerce him and scooped him up when he came flying over to me wagging his tail.

"Grab his dry food from the cupboard," I said. "In case we're in there for a few hours. The noise of the pounding had stopped but out of the corner of my eye I saw a shadow pass by the sliding doors, making my breathing hitch. We should call for help, but who? The cops might do more harm than good.

"We can't call the cops. My ID might not stand up to that kind of scrutiny," Sadie said like she was reading my mind. "What if they discover the truth, Katie, what then? Or maybe it's time to stop this? I've lived with this for so long and it's not getting any easier." Sadie suddenly looked defeated, like the load was crushing the life out of her.

"We don't have to call the police. He'll give it up eventually. Sleep it off. You can't give up, Sadie, I won't let you. I let you down once before, never again."

Andy gave a bark of protest and I realized I was holding him a bit too tightly. I petted his silky head by way of apology.

"We need to move now, Sadie. Grab the food, please."

She did as I asked and we hurried through the living room toward sanctuary. This would be the first time I actually tested out the room in an emergency. But I was not worried about anyone being able to break into it. Made of reinforced concrete it would take a jackhammer many hours to break though it. Though small and cramped, it did feature two stacked bunk beds and a chemical toilet hidden behind a curtain.

"Hold Andy." I plopped his pliant body into Sadie's arms. "Shoot, I forgot the water jug."

"Where is it?"

"Out in the hallway. I'll be right back." My heart rate increased. Why didn't I do it earlier when it was so much easier and safer?

I hurried to the back of the house near the kitchen to retrieve the heavy blue bottle, picked it up and began lumbering through the living room. It was then I heard the noise. Like someone knocked out a pane of glass. Had Quinton decided to go that far? Break in looking for Ashley? I made myself go as fast as possible carrying the ten-liter water jug. Leaving it behind was not an option. No running water in the safe room spelled disaster.

The sounds of pursuit froze the marrow in my bones. Someone was inside the house. Nearby. I found the strength to run then, the water bottle threatening to fall from my hands as I awkwardly cradled it low on my stomach. My legs pumped at the certainty of Quinton only being a few steps behind. The sensation of being almost grabbed focused my fear, expecting any second to be accosted by the brute of a man.

I barreled straight into the safe room, tossing the jug. Praying it didn't break the brittle plastic housing as it rolled off into a corner, I slammed the door shut, automatically engaging the lock.

Too close. *Far too close.* My heart hammered in my chest as if it was going to misfire at any moment. A muffled pounding erupted on the outside of the door. But I knew nothing was getting through that solid steel.

I turned around to find three sets of eyes staring at me.

"That was scary," Sadie whispered.

"Was it Quinton?" Ashley asked, her complexion bleaching to white.

"Had to be. Who else would have just broken in?" I took a moment to gather myself, then went to check on the water container that could have cost me dearly. Maybe even my life? The bottle had cracked along one seam. I needed to stop up the leak. What did I have on hand? Duct tape would work.

I rummaged in the small supply box and found a half a roll along with the emergency medical aid kit and some granola bars and snacks. Then used a towel to sop up the worst of the water and quickly applied a length of tape, cutting it off the roll with a small pair of scissors. I took several more strips of tape before it stopped the water from escaping. Sitting back on my heels, Andy came over and licked my face.

I petted his head and down his back to reassure him in firm strokes. "It's okay. We're safe in here, bud."

"I'm so sorry. I've brought you nothing but trouble," Ashley wailed, tears rolling down her face.

"No need to apologize. We're here for you, Ashley," Sadie said, her expression filled with empathy for the young girl's plight as she handed her a tissue.

"We should all sit down," I said as I slid down the wall

with my back to the wall, thankful the floor was covered by a thick area rug. "Take the bunk."

Instead, the pair of them sat crossed legged on the floor in front of me, their backs pressed to the bunks.

Andy lay down by my side, a true comfort. It would seem we were out on a camping trip if it wasn't for the god-awful fact that a strange man with proven violent tendencies now had full access to my home.

I couldn't help asking the thought aloud, "What do you think he will do?"

Ashley's bottom lip trembled as she blotted at her eyes with the tissue. "I don't know. He's never done anything like this before."

"What does he do for a living?" I asked. So far I'd not seen the pair keep regular hours that suggested any other job or jobs other than housesitting.

The girl looked away and didn't return my eye contact.

"Does he take things?" Sadie asked quietly, both of us obviously thinking it was a possibility. She pretended like it was a normal, everyday conversation.

"You mean steal, right, because we look like trash!"

CHAPTER 15
KATIE

MONDAY 7:33 P.M.

I inwardly groaned. "You don't look like trash, Ashley."

"But you think Quinton does, right? That he'd rob you blind now that he has the opportunity?"

"How well do you know him? Have you two been together long?" Sadie asked to change the subject.

I slapped my forehead as the sudden realization hit. "What was I thinking! There's a camera system installed, wired into the house, so we can check on what he's up to."

Ashley's eyes flew wide open with alarm. "You can do that? We can see him in here?"

"Yes, we can." I scrambled to my feet and unlatched the door that housed the display monitor for the system. "Not that I have anything of much value anyway," I said without forethought.

"What? You have a Warhol. It's got to be worth a pretty penny!" Ashley said, her eyes expressing disbelief.

I didn't want to burst her bubble. It was nice, her

thinking I owned an original, but it was all a lie just like I'd already explained, a screen print worth far less. Why didn't she believe me? Because my gut was telling me that Quinton would use this opportunity to rob me. No qualms attached. I did need to get hold of Daniel though and warn him. I slammed myself for not doing it earlier. My only excuse was it had been a very busy, very trying day. But still, I should have made time. Big question was would the cell phone even work in the bunker? I had no idea as it was encased in cement. I'd try calling him soon as I booted the system to check on Quinton.

"I'm sorry you had to sell your Warhol," Sadie said. "That was wrong of your ex. Brad made you do it, right, so you could keep the house? The only way to raise enough funds to pay him off. And then he takes off with Andy." Sadie shook her head, her face a study in disgust. "At least he's back where he belongs, eh, boy."

Andy opened one eye, wagging his tail. He was the only one who looked relaxed.

Ashley was very quiet, biting on the skin around her fingernails as she digested Sadie's words. "Are you telling me the Warhol's a fake? Quinton's going to be so pissed."

"Why? Are you saying what I think you're saying?" Sadie asked, her glance narrowed at the young girl.

"Are you in on it?" I asked, my stomach dropping. I didn't see this coming.

"What? No." Ashley shook her head vehemently back and forth. But something told me not to believe her. Then the worst idea of all hit. Was this all a scam? Was she only pretending to be abused? No, that couldn't be right. She had all the hallmarks of an abused person.

Then Ashley's shoulders slumped forward in defeat. "I'm sorry. He made me do it. If I didn't help, he said he'd hurt me real bad. Hurt you guys too." Her eyes implored for understanding. "Please, don't be mad at me. I didn't mean you any harm. I figured you had insurance or something."

She looked to be telling the truth. She shone with sincerity. If she was lying, she would have to be an off-the-chart psychopathic personality to pull the wool over our eyes so completely.

"This only proves you need to get away from him before the baby comes," Sadie stepped in, the lines in her face heightened by determination.

Ashley shook her head. "You don't understand. He'll kill me if I leave. He said, if he can't be with me, no one will."

The stark, oppressive words were out in the open. No taking them back.

"You can go where he can't find you. Because if you stay, you might lose your baby. Can you live with that? If he hurts the baby?"

Dead silence as the young girl processed my friend's words. Then she found her voice.

"No. Quinton would never hurt our baby!"

"Tell that to the thousands of women who have lost their lives. Or their children's lives because they didn't leave an abuser in time. You need to think this through, Ashley. If he's hit once, he'll hit again. And saying he will kill you? Believe it."

I turned away to finish dealing with the security system, to give her time to think.

The screen came to life as I clicked the remote access, divided into eight images with feeds from the cameras located around the house. Unfortunately, one square stayed black, indicative of something having gone wrong with the camera or the connections. Everything was hard wired into the home, something I appreciated, not having to worry about battery life. We did get fairly decent views of the front of the house from the camera pointed outward at the front step, one in the kitchen, another two in the huge living room, one in the back hallway, one in the formal dining room and one by the pool.

Yes. Quinton was occupied at the moment removing the fake Warhol. He cut it from the frame then rolled it up while I watched. Did he not know that doing that with original artwork may render it of lesser value due to possible damage? Especially if it has an old veneer coating that could crack, like the unrecovered Rembrandts and the Vermeer taken in the Gardner heist decades ago. The Warhol didn't have that type of finish, but cut from the frame it was smaller and less attractive to a buyer. What was I going on about? He was a thief, and not a gentleman thief, but an abuser of women. The worst kind of man.

"What do you know?" Ashley said with derision, her tone defensive. "Quinton helped me when no one else cared. Got me off the streets. Looks after me. Sure, he's not perfect, but it beats being all alone. Especially now I'm pregnant."

"What part of this are you not getting, Ashley?" Sadie said, her exasperation clear. "You think we have no idea of what you've been through?"

"What? You've been abused?"

Sadie said nothing, her face filled with torment. I knew she was warring with herself. Wanting to say she knew more about this than she ever wanted to know. But Sadie hated talking about the past. It hurt her right to the depths of her being. Reliving it was a nightmare all over again and could spiral her right back into the depths of the deepest, darkest depression. For her to help

Ashley, it would be painful beyond measure. And if the girl won't listen, why should my friend suffer such torment?

"I thought not."

"You don't know what you're talking about, Ashley," I said, intervening. I couldn't have my friend attacked for no good reason.

The young girl sniffed her displeasure. "I know enough. Once the baby comes Quinton will be fine. You guys are manhaters, right? Freaking women libbers. Everything's always their fault, right. Never the woman's. Well, I'm not perfect and I'm not afraid to say so. I even had him write a list to help me become a better person. I have proof. It's not all Quinton's fault."

She tugged a piece of folded paper out of her sundress pocket and held it out. "See."

I took it from her and smoothed out the page. Began reading it aloud. "Ashley's Self-Improvement List: Never let anyone know any details about us. Don't talk back to the Top Dog. Always smile when you're with the Top Dog. Be a perfect girlfriend for the Top Dog. If the Top Dog asks for a drink, bring him one quick with a smile. Remember you're stupid without me. Remember—" My mouth dropped open. "What the hell is this, Ashley?"

"It helps me."

"Being told what to do helps you? Well, if that's the case. I'm telling you *leave* this guy immediately. He's working to tear you down, not build you up. What he wrote here disgusts me." I crunched up the paper and threw it away with scorn.

"You can't do that! I have a right to choose how I live my life. Who I live with."

"You may have at one time. No more," Sadie said.

94

"Not when you have an innocent new life depending on you."

"How are you going to handle prenatal care, moving around so much?" I asked, trying to get her to see logistics if nothing else. "Your body is going to go through a lot of chances. You'll need monitoring by a doctor. Vitamins and proper nutrition. Proper rest and care. It all costs money. Can Quinton provide it all?"

"He will. Not like I can't help too. He cares about me. You don't know everything. Not like either of you know what it's like to love someone so much you're willing to change, to be what they need. To care more about them than anything else in the world."

Ashley was deluding herself if she thought things were going to get better. Add the stress of a newborn to a problematic relationship and there's no telling what can happen. New babies and telling them you're leaving for good, two sure-fire methods to bring out the aggressor in a battering male.

"Do you have any idea how many women have told themselves that lie? Quinton has to own his shit first, then, and only then, can he be a good husband and father," Sadie said, shaking her head in a telling way.

The girl was pushing all our buttons. She had no idea what she was letting herself in for. She was altruistic after all, exactly what a bad boy like Quinton counted on. Maybe he was even the one in twenty-five of us that scientists believe have psychopathic tendencies; people born without a conscience. We'd not separated as much by intelligence, race, or gender as much as we were isolated from understanding those who live among us without a conscience. I'm not saying that Quinton was a sociopath, I wasn't a specialist in the disorder, only an interested party having researched to gain some understanding of what drives people to criminal acts against their partners. But hard questions needed to be asked. There was a checklist thought I might casually bring up with Ashley, see if he hit enough of the characteristics to be suspect of the neuropsychiatric disorder. In the meantime, I could point out some of the more obvious concerns she should consider.

"Do you really believe a good man would try to get you to steal for him? Have you act like a decoy? He had you pretend to be hurt, right, or did he really hit you? You can't have it both ways," I asked, deciding what was the point of pussyfooting around the situation.

"He only does that because he has to. Not like anyone's going to give us the money to pay for what we need," Ashley said, two pinpoints of color high on her cheekbones drawing my attention to the darkening bruise over her eye.

"But he did hit you, right? Then tell you to keep us hidden in the safe room I told you about while he stole from me?"

The young girl pressed her lips tight together, unwilling, or afraid to admit to or deny my insinuations.

"You say that we don't understand what it's like. All I can say is, we understand this all too well, far more than you know. Or at least I do."

My gaze flicked to Sadie, and I shook my head ever so slightly at her. *Don't do it unless you want to.* Surely there were other ways to appeal to this girl than to sentence my best friend to relive her nightmares?

CHAPTER 16
ASHLEY

"What do you mean, Sadie?" I asked, surprised and intrigued by her words. Had Sadie been abused by a man? She didn't appear to be the type with her edgy dark hairstyle and her tough stance.

"Oh shoot, I forget!" Katie said, interrupting the flow. "I have to call Daniel Johnson."

"Why do you need to call him?" Sadie asked.

Damn, just as she was about to share something important too. I felt the edges of the electronic device in my pocket finding it comforting. Fully charged with fifty-seven hours of battery life, I could operate this sucker in the dark. It was as good a lifeline as any in the modern world.

"I only wanted to check in on him. See how he's doing." Katie pulled out her cell phone. She had a guilty look now.

"You mean you want to find out if he realizes what kind of people are living in his house, right? You think Quinton and I are abusing his place or something like that?"

"No, what I want to share is how his current house sitters are stealing *my* stuff," Katie warned, her eyes cutting in my direction.

"I explained all of it. I had no choice or something bad would have happened. I did it to protect us." I folded in on myself, my pulse skittering. Why was all this bad stuff happening now?

"I'm not blaming you—I'm blaming Quinton. He's the one that put you up to all this, right?"

Best to say nothing. Adults had taught me the value of saying nothing or denying everything like so many in politics do. This situation was too volatile to call.

"Men. *Can't live with them, can't live without them*," Sadie said. Her expression was one of acute sadness, not the usual glib or irony that I'd seen accompanying the quote. "Sorry about the cliché, but it does happen to be true in a lot of cases."

I watched Katie dealing with her phone. Good luck in reaching Daniel Johnson. He's a bit tied up at the moment. I almost let loose a bark of hysterical laughter before I caught myself. Last thing I needed was to give the game away. Whatever sympathy I had managed to elicit today would vanish in a heartbeat if they knew the truth. Not that I could blame them, Daniel was an innocent bystander in all this.

"No answer." Katie threw her phone done in disgust. "Went straight to voice mail. I sent him a text though so hopefully he'll answer soon."

"I'm surprised you got a signal," Sadie said. "The walls in this room are really thick and made of reinforced cement, right?"

"Cement?" I said, looking around wildly, the word near choking me as it escaped my windpipe. The painted gyprock hid what the room was actually made of.

Another confined space from years ago forced itself back into my mind. I was locked inside a gray-colored room. Unable to escape. The cold, dreary walls squeezing in on me while I waited for my punishment to be over. What had I done to earn it? Nothing, it had been the daughter of the house who had stolen the candy bars, not me. But her mother thought her precious Evelyn, Susan's far luckier sister, could do no wrong so she blamed me. The easy scapegoat. Susan had been lucky to escape that time. Maybe blood had mattered more? Susan was adopted after all while I was only a foster kid.

"What is it, Ashley? What's wrong?"

I pressed my lips together. Attempted to gather myself. "Not a fan of confined spaces. I didn't realize how difficult it would be to break out of here if the door wouldn't open." Beads of sweat pooled on my lower back, dampening my dress.

"I'm sure when Quinton's done robbing me, he'll leave. Why hang around and take the chance someone will discover what he's been up to?" Katie said, obviously trying to reassure me. It didn't work.

"Who might come around?" I asked suspiciously. Was something else planned I didn't know about? This was such a bad idea. If what we were up to was discovered now, this close to my goal, I would lose my chance. I sensed the window of opportunity about to slam shut behind me.

"No one specific. But I'm not a hermit. My ex was already by once today. A neighbor might hear something —come over to investigate."

"Quinton's got a gun," I blurted.

Two sets of horrified eyes stared at me.

"It's for protection," I said with a shrug. "The business he's in, it can be dangerous. He needs to keep us safe."

99

"Business of robbing people? Call it what it is," Sadie said, the corners of her mouth curving downward.

"Have you seen him use it? The gun?" Katie asked.

"No, of course not! He just has it to make people do what he wants. He'd never shoot anybody intentionally."

"Are you sure about that?" Sadie's expression held disbelief.

"So what's his plan? Is it a quick in and out job? Will he be gone soon?" Katie asked.

Damn, she would have to ask that. "He didn't share it with me. I guess. I don't know why he'd want to hang around afterward."

"I know why. He'd stay to accost you—to make you go with him. Are you going to do that, Ashley, go back to him?" Sadie asked, her eyes narrowed as she kept up the intense scrutiny. What was her problem?

"I don't know." I averted my eyes, finding her continued stare annoying. "Maybe?"

"What would it take for you to see how wrong it would be?"

Was she asking me or was it meant figuratively? Sadie had finally quit staring at me, leaning back on the bunk, seeming lost in thought.

"I guess knowing how someone else handled things like this, you know, did all right afterward, that might help?" I said tentatively, recognizing it for what it was. The chance to learn the truth. My heart rate jacked up. Was she going to explain something that would be a game changer?

"Someone's at the front door," Katie said. "Oh no, it's Brad."

CHAPTER 17
KATIE

MONDAY 7:45 P.M.

"What is Brad doing back?" I asked, staring at the monitor. If only I could warn him. Tell him to go away. That a dangerous man lurked on the other side of that door. Thoughts of how this could go bad in an instant made my skin crawl with alarm. My headache bloomed again, causing a sensation of knife points stabbing at my brain. My vision narrowed. I wanted desperately to run out of the room and warn him, but I couldn't expose Sadie and Ashley to what could come next if I were to be so foolish as to expose them to Quinton's wrath.

I watched the pantomime as Brad looked to be shouting at the house. Was he that upset about losing Andy? A bit of sympathy I didn't want to feel crept in. He had to have been drinking to be acting that way. I hoped he hadn't driven over. Was Willow outside waiting for him? I couldn't see the driveway and I had missed the vehicle pulling up. Note to self, after this ordeal is over get more cameras for around the property.

"What's Quinton doing?" Sadie asked, getting to her feet and joining me at the monitor. Then all three of us pressed in close to observe what would happen next.

"Go away, Brad!" I half-shouted at the screen though he couldn't hear me.

"Oh no! Quinton's opening the bloody door," Sadie said, her hand pressed over her mouth in horror.

Not being able to do anything, standing there helpless, there was no word for how low it made me feel. I was stuck watching the initial surprise on Brad's face when Quinton greeted him. A brief discussion, then Quinton stepping back, inviting him in.

"Why did he do that?" I groaned, holding my head in my hands. Sadie laid a comforting hand on my shoulder.

"Quinton won't hurt him."

I whirled on the young girl. "You don't know that. He has a gun for heaven's sake!"

"Why do you care so much? Not like he's your husband anymore."

I was within a heartbeat of slapping the silly girl. I wanted to scream, wake up! Counting to ten helped me refocus. How could I think of touching Ashley? What was wrong with me? My nerves jangled with disbelief that I had even had such a deplorable thought. The young girl couldn't help it. She'd been brainwashed by a narcissist monster.

I couldn't bear to watch what was happening on the monitor, but there was no other choice. I had to know. Was Brad going to be okay? And what if Willow drove over with him, things would get even more dicey if she tried to come in.

Helpless, we stayed glued to the screen. Brad crossed the living room floor to the sofa. He sat down while Quinton went into the kitchen and poured a couple of drinks, clearly shown in the second camera. Quinton then reached into his pocket and opened a vial, placing a few drops of a clear substance in one of the beer glasses.

"Is he drugging Brad?" I said, my eyes disbelieving what I was seeing.

"No biggie. Just that date rape drug. You know, the one that caused the funny scenes in the movie *Hangover*," Ashley said so calmly I wanted to shake some sense into her. Her callous comment raised a big red flag for me. Were her views that warped from being with the guy? Chilling, if so.

"No biggie! My god, Ashley, that's so wrong!" Sadie said, shaking her head. "This isn't a damn movie. It's real life. People die of overdoses all the time." Then my friend caught sight of my horrified expression and added, "I'm sorry, Katie. I wasn't thinking. I'm sure he'll be fine."

"You don't know that." My head began to pound, and I swayed drunkenly on my feet.

"My goodness, Katie. You need to sit down," Sadie said, taking my arm.

"I'm fine. It's Brad who's in trouble. We're safe in here while he's out there dealing with a freaking psycho." I turned on Ashley before she had a chance to say anything. "And don't deny it. Actions do speak louder than words, missy."

To her credit the young girl clammed up.

Quinton brought the beers back into the living room, handing one off to Brad. It was like watching a horror movie in real time. We couldn't do anything about it while the villain calmly went about doing his damage. Brad pointed at spot where the Warhol should be, his expression bemused, making me wonder what the hell was being said. But I had to do something to stop this train wreck.

"There's a gun in here," I said. "Or a least there used to be." I had an innate mistrust of guns though I did know how to use one and was considered a good shot, having learned as a teenager by taking a Hunter's Safety course offered by our municipality and going to so-called Turkey Shoots where the closest bullet to the bull's eyes on a stationary target won a turkey. But I was also well aware that a weapon in a home was as much a danger to the homeowners as to anyone thinking to harm them. I tore open the lid of the supply box and rummaged around for the telltale black zippered case that held the Glock.

"But you can't go out there. It's too dangerous, Katie," Sadie said.

"She's right. You could get hurt or worse," Ashley said. "I'm sorry, this is all my fault. Quinton shouldn't have given him the drug. He's not thinking straight, it's wrong to do that."

At least Ashley was appearing to be seeing things in a more clear-headed fashion. If she woke up at least some good could come yet of this terrifying situation.

I found the gun and hunched back on my heels, aware of the weight of it. It seemed far too light for the harm it could do. I unzipped the case and pulled it out, the black metal gleaming dully in the overhead lighting. I tentatively pulled it out. Was it loaded? I checked the chamber and found it was ready for action.

"Look, Quinton's just tying Brad up. He's not shooting him or anything," Ashley said, her voice sounding relieved.

I set the gun aside and returned to watching the monitor. Brad was lying on the sofa now, his hands tied behind his back. Quinton pulled the colorful crocheted afghan I always kept on the back of it for impromptu naps and threw it over his captive, leaving his face uncovered.

"Do you think he needs medical help?" I asked. I zoomed the camera feed in on Brad, noticed that his chest was rising and falling softly. "He's breathing fine at least."

"I think we should hold off doing anything for now," Sadie said.

"And Quinton will probably leave soon and take the stuff he wants with him," Ashley added. "Let's wait a little longer, okay? I don't want to see anyone get hurt."

"Why did he have to come back here tonight? He had to know Andy's doing great, that I'll take good care of him." Brad wasn't usually so impulsive. At least not when I had known him. Maybe Willow had something to do with it? Memories of his insistence of things being done in a certain order came back to me. I had admired that about him. It had meant I could rely on him to plan vacations to perfection, keep our finances in order, preparing for any contingency. Of course, that meant he knew our exact worth and used that against me in the divorce. What had come between us? My housing a dark secret had been at the root cause of it if I was being honest. He always accused me of holding something back. Of making him feel unsettled not knowing what I was thinking during those times when I was being affected by nightmares, reliving those terrible moments all over again. Something I could never share with another living human being.

I'd spent a lot of energy downplaying it, saying it was a childhood affliction that I'd been told I'd grow out of. Just teased that it only proved I still had a lot of growing up to do. When Brad and I were good, we were really good. Our love had created a force field around us, a sanctuary of extraordinary protective power, and when he'd cheated and ended up leaving after my inability to forgive him, I had mourned the loss of the protective power as much as anything. Seeing him in the clutches of a monster made me unsettled, unrooted more than the day he'd walked out. Made me want to run screaming into the living room, gun in hand. Be the hero of the story.

"My guess is he's missing this little guy." Sadie reached down and gave Andy a good scratching behind the ears. Andy basked in the attention, preening his head, eyes closed in contentment. At least he was unaffected by all this.

My anger at Brad had lessened considerably, seeing him in acute danger. Much as I hated what he had done to me, to us, I didn't want to see him hurt in any fashion. Well, maybe just his dignity when I hit him with the pie. That I had to own up to. "Do you think Willow's outside?"

"Best if she's not. What can she do except cause more problems."

The earlier alcohol had worn off and my thirst returned with a vengeance. "Anyone need a drink? I have glasses in the supply kit." I dug out three bright red cups normally used for informal parties and handed them over.

"Hold still while I fill them." It was awkward dealing with the huge and all too heavy water bottle, but I managed to fill all three cups and a water bowl for Andy.

"I have granola bars and snacks." I pulled those out as well and threw them down on the bottom bunk so everyone could help themselves. We needed a break from all the tension and stress. Maybe eating would help give us all a better perspective on things. If nothing else, it would pass some time.

Munching and sipping the water did fill up a few minutes. But I barely took my eyes off the camera feed that showed Brad still sleeping. I needed to see that he kept breathing. *Just breathe, Brad.*

. . . .*

CHAPTER 18
ASHLEY

"Before her ex arrived." I nodded at Katie. "You were going to share something important. You asked me what it would take to change my mind about being with Quinton? Like you'd been through something in your life, Sadie?" I hesitated for a moment, wondering how best to phrase it to find out what I needed to know. "Was that what you meant? You knew something that might help me make a decision?"

Sadie looked at me, her expression making her appear undecided about whether or not she should share.

"I would think you already know the right thing to do, Ashley. The writing's on the wall," Katie said, making me angry at her interference. Couldn't she just let her friend speak for herself? I sensed Sadie could help me if I could find the words to get her to spill what she knew.

"You think this is easy? I want to do the right thing, okay, I just don't know what that is. I'm carrying Quinton's baby. Doesn't he have rights too?"

"No, he doesn't. Not the way he is now," Sadie said.

"He can still change. Don't you believe in second chances?" I asked.

"*Fool me once, shame on you*. You don't want to be fooled by him a second time, Ashley, it will only bring shame to you and possible harm to your baby," Katie said.

"I'm going to share something with you that you need to hear, Ashley," Sadie said, making my pulse skitter. *Yes. Please.*

"Tell me."

"I mean *really* hear. Not just give lip service to."

"I promise." I reached into my pocket and tugged out a tissue. I blew my nose and threw it in the small garbage container with the retractable lid that bounced upward as I hit the lever.

"I was once in a situation similar to you," she said.

I remained quiet, letting her know she had my full attention.

"I was expecting, just like you. Only further along, seven months. I wanted my baby, oh so much, I can't tell you how much. I had dreams of offering her a better life than I had." Sadie gave a touching smile that didn't reach her eyes. She didn't look as happy about having a baby as you'd expect her to be. Why? Did she turn out to be a bad mother?

"A girl," I blurted out. "Like me."

"You know that already?"

Had I made a mistake? "I meant just like I want to have. I want a girl too. Of course, Quinton wants a boy."

"Well, long as they're healthy, right?" Katie said.

I nodded eagerly. "Right."

"How old is your daughter now?" I asked, turning back to Sadie. She looked even sadder now if that were possible.

"She'll never get any older. She died when she was a day old. Born too early with a heart defect they couldn't fix."

"I'm so sorry. That's terrible." The news floored me, made me want to know more.

"Let me tell her about that first night, Sadie, when it rained," Katie said.

Sadie's eyes filled with tears, but she nodded her acceptance, making my spirits sink again. Damn Katie for interrupting again.

"We'd all come back from the funeral, from the graveyard. It had been a terrible day as you can imagine. The day we buried Sadie's daughter. Overcast, cold, like the whole world was grieving the loss of Josie Mary Katherine."

"What a beautiful name," I murmured.

"I named her after my mother and grandmother," Sadie said.

"What about the father? Did he like that name too?"

"He had no say in it by then," Sadie said, her eyes filled with bitterness.

"Why, what did he do?"

"Let me finish my story first, Ashley," Katie said, a touch of impatience in her tone at my questioning Sadie.

My own frustration at wanting answers only grew, but I made the universal zipping-my-lips gesture to create some peace.

I received a hard look from Katie for my efforts and felt my skin heat, fearing I had appeared gauche.

"Then while we stood around the funeral hall having some refreshments, it began pouring rain. A torrential downfall that battered the roof of the building like the gods were angry too. They had a right to be. It was a terrible tragedy that could have been avoided."

"What are you saying? Did somebody do something?" I was totally confused now. "It's no one's fault when a baby is born with a defect. Unless the mother didn't take vitamins or something?"

Katie went on like I hadn't interrupted. It was all I could manage not to demand to know exactly what had happened. "Sadie got upset. She tore out of the building, racing to her car. I caught up to her, wanting to take her back inside. She was drenched and shaking. There was a lightning strike nearby and a tree was hit and caught on fire, illuminating the torment on her face. I was terrified she was going to get killed and I urged her to come back inside. To stay safe. She pushed me away and opened the trunk of the car, and pulled out a blue plastic tarp and a blanket used for picnics. I'll never forget what she said next, I wake up at nights hearing it over and over." Katie stopped and took a deep breath, her eyes clouded with the memory. "She said, 'I'm her mother. I have to cover Josie. She's cold and wet.'" Tears escaped Katie's eyes and her face turned blotchy with stark red patches.

A second later Katie was rushing to embrace her friend. Sobs filled the claustrophobic feeling room.

I sat shocked, unable to comprehend such a thing.

"I'm so sorry, Sadie. I should have been there sooner for you. It's all my fault."

"It's not your fault. If I hadn't been so convinced he was going to become a better man, a good father, I wouldn't have stayed. There's nothing you could have done. You did all you could. If it wasn't for you, hell, I wouldn't even be here. He would have killed me too."

"Killed you?" I picked up on the insane sounding words. This made no sense at all. They had to be exaggerating things.

No answer to my question, the pair too busy reassuring each other, commiserating. None of this was helping. My questions weren't being answered properly. It was making me feel miserable. And I certainly wasn't going to fall for any of their mind games. Someone in this room was hiding the truth. A darker truth than my own. I just had to figure out how to expose them, and shut up the clock ticking louder and louder.

CHAPTER 19
KATIE

MONDAY 8:10 P.M.

I smoothed back Sadie's hair, revealing her roots. "You need a color job," I said, ignoring the tremor in my voice. "Your blonde's showing through again."

"You dye your hair black?" Ashley asked, screwing up her face like it was a national scandal.

"Been so busy I sort of forgot about it. I'd better do something before I look like a skunk."

My friend's voice trembled as well but speaking of such a mundane thing seemed to help. Sadie wiped her eyes with a tissue, throwing the dark mascara-stained wad in the trash container. I did the same. Letting go by sharing the pain that never left me had helped somewhat. I could only hope it helped Sadie as well. Her pain had to be far worse than mine. In fact, I had no idea how she functioned on a day-to-day basis.

"I'll give you a hand tomorrow if you like?" I offered.

"Thanks. That's if we're free of all this by then."

"Why do you dye your hair black? If I had naturally

blonde hair, I wouldn't dye it. You like goth or some-thing?" Ashley twirled a lock of her own dark-brown hair between her fingers like it was sadly lacking.

Sadie shrugged. "I needed a change at first. Then I discovered dark hair makes it easier to hide in a crowd."

"Huh. Maybe you could dye my hair for me? I'd love to be a blonde and draw attention."

"You have lovely hair. But if you want a big change, I'd be glad to help. Especially if it makes it easier for you to slip away if you're thinking of doing that?" I said, unable to stop myself from making the suggestion.

Ashley didn't answer but seemed to be thinking about it. I truly hoped she was listening to us. Realized the danger she was in. Right about now I was ready to kidnap her and deprogram her like you do after some-one's escaped a nefarious cult. Or was calling a cult *nefarious* redundant? But maybe this time in the safe room, all three of us being candid, was fate's way of helping us help her. I should've perhaps been wishing that Quinton stayed longer, giving us more time to persuade Ashley of the danger she was in. *Brad.* I suddenly remembered what was playing out in the living room and I quickly shifted my gaze to the split-screen of the monitor, double-clicking to bring in the image close enough to check if he was still breathing. Yes. He looked the same. Quinton was nowhere to be seen. Had he left? Afraid to get my hopes up that this siege was about to come to an end, I turned to Ashley, wanting to make one final plea if our time was nearly up.

"I should fill you in on some statistics about battered women I've learned through my work trying to help them while I have the opportunity. Did you know more than sixty percent of violent incidences toward women happen at home between the hours of six p.m. and six a.m.? That women are thirty-three percent more likely to become homeless, that one in three homicides the woman's partner is to blame? That women between the age of twenty and twenty-four are the most likely victims, just around your age? Hundreds of thousands of women are battered every year in Canada alone, four million in the United States. Shocking but true. I'm only telling you this as a wake-up call. Not to make you feel worse, but to get you to realize you have a choice."

"Sometimes it goes the other way, right? Women do things to men too." The girl was back to looking mutinous again and I was stymied by her quick rejection of such dreadful, revealing facts. I had never gone against a woman so hell-bent on her own destruction. Or maybe it was because they only came to me after they had been thinking about it for a while? Maybe this was all new for Ashley? I should be more patient in light of that.

"Eighty-five percent of the perpetrators are male. Females make up a paltry fifteen percent. So, no, it doesn't go the other way very often. Why would you even ask that?" It seemed a strange question for Ashley to be asking. "Are you the one hitting Quinton?"

Ashley turned beet red. "No. But I'm not always a good partner. Sometimes I ask for it."

"What does that mean? You ask for it? Did you slam his head into the floor, cut his Achilles tendon? Did you throw your supper against a wall because you came home late and it had dried out? Did you talk to another male and he went ape-shit on your ass? What? What did you do that deserved getting hit? Tell me that? What did my poor baby do to have to suffer being born too early before she had a chance at life?"

"Is that what happened to you? Is that why you walk

so funny? Sorry, bad choice of words. But you do walk kind of stiff like."

Sadie looked about ready to blow up. Her fists clenched at her sides as she stared at Ashley like she was the enemy instead of Quinton.

"I think we all need to calm down," I said. Things were getting out of hand. Time to stop trying so hard to persuade Ashley of anything. In the end, we all have to choose our destiny. I couldn't do it for her. I could only try to help and pray she saw the light in time to save herself.

"It's not going to help for me to leave Quinton," Ashley said so softly I could barely hear her. "He'd find me. I tried once before, you know, but he still found me. Even though I went to the cops and got a court injunction. There's nothing either of you can do for me. I'm doomed. He'd hurt you both if he knew what you are trying to get me to do. The only way Quinton would leave me alone is if he's dead. You're lucky, Sadie, that the guy you had a kid with has left you alone all these years. That won't be the case with me. But thanks, I appreciate what you are trying to do here, trying to help me. But I can't ask you to do that. It will only put you in danger too."

"Oh, Ashley, I'm so sorry!" Sadie said, her expression equal parts horrified and guilty.

"You know, if it's self-defense, a jury may find you innocent of the crime. Hell, you might not be charged," I said, planting the seed. Maybe she would have the strength to fight back one day when she needed to the most. I'd once had a cop say to one of the women I tried to help that if a woman hit an abuser over the head with a poker when he was hurting him, he'd agree that it was self-defense as would most lawmen.

"You mean pick a fight then hit him with a hammer or something?"

Hammer. Why did she have to suggest something so specific? The image her words brought up sent me spiraling right back to that awful day. A day that would live in infamy. Two days before Josie was born. And what happened in that time before Merri, who later became known as Sadie, gave birth to her. The events that left her disabled, in body and spirit.

———

NINE YEARS AGO

It had been a Saturday night, around three in the morning when Merri had called me. At first, I could barely understand her, she was so upset and speaking so softly, like she didn't want anyone to overhear her.

"Please, I need you, Katie. Come now...bathroom, door locked."

I recognized only that she was in trouble and needed me. I came wide awake in an instant, even though I had only been in bed an hour or two having been at a party in town, a pre-celebration for grad. "I'm coming. Stay on the line, okay?"

"I can't." The lifeline between us went dead in my hands, making me swear aloud.

I clamored out of bed and hurriedly dressed in jeans and a sweatshirt, not bothering with socks, but pushed my bare feet into my old sneakers.

Not wanting to wake my mother, who was not the deepest sleeper, I crept down the stairs, making sure to avoid the ones that creaked. I grabbed my bike from the garage and took off like a shot toward the small trailer on the edge of town where Sadie had been living with Wyatt the last few months. Since she and Wyatt had been together, I had been seeing less and less of my best friend I'd been paired at the hip with since starting kindergarten. But she was expecting a baby girl, so maybe she just didn't have the same time for me. It hurt a lot. Couldn't say it didn't. But I sucked it up most days, knowing I was leaving town soon anyway for college. Growing up had been proving to be painful if you lost your best friend along the way. But she'd called me when she needed help, no one else, so she still cared.

I was always considered the more level-headed of the two of us, everyone said so. Merri was made of gentler stuff, more refined, while I was never afraid of life, always tackling things head on. It had taken years to learn to control myself better. That night though, what loomed ahead, changed me, taught a life lesson I wouldn't wish on my worst enemy.

When the trailer came into view, I found it in complete darkness. Only the glow of the hydro light near the road lit up the end of the dirt driveway that led onto the property. Had the electricity gone off? I tried to remember the layout. The bathroom was next to the spare room, the one that Ashley was working hard to turn into the nursery. She was working as a cashier at the Co-op, saving every dime to pay for a second-hand crib and baby stuff. A shower was planned soon, before Josie was born, the name she planned to call her baby daughter.

I redialed her number, but it went straight to voice mail. No other choice, I had to get inside to see if Merri was okay. Deciding to go around back of the mobile home, I counted the windows to the bathroom, then stepped in closer only to realize it was above my head and I couldn't see inside. I grabbed an old milk crate lying on its side and stood on it and it was enough of a boost for me to be able to see through the small window. It was too dark to make out much. I held my phone up to act like a flashlight and there was Merri huddled on the floor, her big belly looking like a watermelon under her thin, cotton house dress.

She lumbered to her feet when she saw me and came to the window, sliding it open.

"Are you okay?" I asked. Closer up, I could see that her lip was swollen and bleeding.

"Yeah, I think so," she whispered back.

A lone wolf howled in the distance, sending chills racing down my spine. A moment later the pack answered the call, making my paranoia kick in. Which would be worse, being attacked by a human or a hungry wolf pack? I had no time for either, needing to help my friend above all.

"We got to get you out of here. Where's Wyatt at?" I kept my voice low as well, not wanting to be ambushed by the guy.

"I'm not sure. He pounded on the door for a while, then he left. But I didn't hear his motorcycle, so he may have passed out in the living room. He was drunk. It's Saturday night." She said that like it excused his deplorable behavior.

"I'm coming in. I'll head around front and help you get out, okay?"

"Be careful. He was in a bad mood earlier." Merri bit her lip, like she wanted to say more.

"Don't worry. I won't take any shit from him." My words were filled with more courage than I actually felt, the wolves having nearly unseated me visioning being attacked by something or someone, but I wanted my friend to know I had her back.

Balancing myself against the aluminum siding of the trailer, I stepped off the crate, then crept around to the front porch. A sledgehammer lay propped up against the side of the building. It was a smaller version than most, but it looked useful enough. Without thinking, I picked it up and slowly turned the doorknob. It was unlocked, and I slipped inside.

I took a few seconds to allow my eyes to adjust to the darkness of the living room. Where was Wyatt? I could see no human shape on the sofa or anywhere in the room. Maybe he had left? Just went for a walk instead of taking his bike. But I couldn't count on it. I raised the sledgehammer and allowed it to rest on my shoulder. It helped, made me feel invincible.

Very slowly, I walked down the narrow hall that led to the bedrooms and small bathroom. In front of the door that I knew Merri hid behind, I knocked softly.

"It's me, Katie. You can come out now," I whispered.

The door began to open. But before I could grab Merri's hand a body slammed into me, knocking me sideways. I hit the floor hard enough to knock the air from my lungs. Too stunned for a moment to move, I finally found my voice and yelled, "What the hell did you do that for?"

Then I realized it was Wyatt who loomed over me, his face twisted by rage, his breath stinking of liquor. The weapon had fallen from my nerveless fingers and lay at my side. He had Merri by the arm, her body half-turned away from me as she struggled to get free of him, to run toward the back of the trailer. But I knew she'd be trapped back there with no back door. It had been blocked off with plywood after Wyatt had broken it one night, trying to get in.

"Let me go!" she screamed. He hit her then, making her cry out in pain. "Stop, you'll hurt Josie."

I couldn't let him hurt her. Not Merri, the gentlest, kindest person I knew. She was only with this asshole because she felt sorry for him, certain she could fix what was wrong with him. Make up for his years of feeling abused by his father.

"Stop hurting her!" I shouted, only adding to the din. It did no good, he kept dragging Merri away. My ears buzzed with white noise. I was so angry my vision narrowed. I could only see the monster stealing my friend. It was then I saw the knife he pulled from his back pocket. He held it to behind her, then reached down and cut at the back of one ankle.

"You'll never run from me again, bitch," he said as the blood flowed from the wound.

Merri slumped, the fight gone from her. What had he done? Shock and adrenaline forced me to my feet, my body powered by a superhuman strength. I grabbed the sledgehammer by instinct, raised it over his head. I brought it down with all my might. A terrible cracking sound like an egg being broken into a pan and the monster fell backward onto the linoleum floor.

"Oh no! Wyatt! Is he dead?" Merri asked, crawling over to where I was checking on him. I could hardly bear to touch him, my disgust at the whole situation making my stomach roil.

"No, he's still breathing." Then I turned away and threw up.

———

PRESENT DAY

"Just so you know. I could never do that. Hit Quinton with anything," Ashley said.

With my mind still consumed by the memory of what happened in the past, it took a few seconds to gather myself, to comprehend the meaning of the words she'd spoken.

"You okay, Katie?" Sadie asked. When I looked over at her, I still saw Merri in my mind. Her blonde hair spilling out over her narrow shoulders around a face filled by pain and grief. Her body shuddering with pain, her ankle bleeding profusely.

"Yeah, I'm okay," I finally managed to squeak out though I was as far from okay as I could be. I took a few deep breaths, trying to control the nausea to stop myself from throwing up what little was in my stomach. I felt shaky, like I was coming down with something that makes your bones achy and your head stuff up like it's filled with cotton wool.

"Here, have some water," Sadie said, handing me a glassful.

"Thanks." I gave my friend a grateful look.

"How long you guys known each other?" Ashley asked. "You said you were both from the same home-town, right?"

"All our lives. Besties growing up—still are," Sadie said with a smile.

I had to figure out a way to get through to Ashley, cling to that idea of getting through to her. For the wistful look on her face as Sadie shared our history about cracked my heart in two.

CHAPTER 20
ASHLEY

"Let's try a little test, shall we. You up for it, Ashley?" Katie asked, giving me a penetrating look. She was paler now, like she been through something in the past few minutes when she zoned out.

Instantly suspicious, I asked, "What kind of test? What's this all about?" Back to game playing so soon? The story of Sadie's baby had bothered me more than I cared to admit. I shook my head. No way would that happen to me. To us. To my precious little daughter.

"You'd like to know if Quinton's father material, right, before the baby's born? I can help you make that decision. That's if you want to protect your baby girl."

I wrapped my arms around my middle, hugging myself. "He's trying his best to look out for me and our baby. Leaving him will only makes things worse so no point in going there if that's where this is headed. But sure, if it will make you feel better, I'll play along."

"Well, we already know he fails to conform to social norms due to his robbing people's homes while they're hiding in a safe room. So that's one of seven characteristics that suggest his mental state. Would you say he's impulsive as well, fails to plan ahead?"

"His mental state? What are you getting at? And sure, he's impulsive, but then so are lots of people. Doesn't mean they're mental. Yeah, he's an outlaw, but lots of women have tamed bad boys."

"Added to some other qualifiers, it might mean a person has issues, falls under the psychopathy umbrella."

"Are you calling Quinton a psycho?" I nearly called her a bitch, but held my tongue. How dare she! Her calm demeanor was only driving up my own anger. Telling me to leave him was one thing, calling him a psycho was something else entirely. Not that I knew all that much about the condition. But enough to know he couldn't be one. They became serial killers and the like, right? Like Bundy and the clown guy. Quinton was just twisted like me from how hard our childhoods were. Doesn't make either of us a psychopath.

"I don't have enough data or a degree in psychology to make that determination. But if he hits at least three of the seven characteristics on the checklist developed by a Canadian university professor, then you got to at least consider it."

"What are the others?" I gave her the side eye, wanting nothing more than to escape this stupid room. How much longer was this going to take?

"Does he worry about your safety? Has he done anything that made you feel afraid for your life?"

I chewed on a strip of flesh around one of my fingernails, considering her question. Which time did she mean? The ones where he drove too fast, nearly spilling us off his hog. Lots of race drivers drive too fast. Or when he threatened me? But that always changed soon as he sobered up. I lived for those times when he was so sweet to me, giving me little gifts and trying to be nice. But the worst time came to the forefront, the one that still haunted me. The one that had made me go to the cops to ask what I could do to stop him.

"Slow down!" I screamed. But my voice was taken away by the rushing wind. We were flying down the Trans-Canada Highway, heading for Winnipeg. We passed through a low-lying cloud and condensation instantly coated my helmet making it difficult to see. I couldn't take a chance at wiping it away from my visor, I was clinging on for dear life to Quinton's muscular waist.

When he swerved to avoid a frost boil created from the spring thaw, we had careened to the left, and it was the longest few seconds of my life before the Harley somehow corrected itself, going over the solid white line in the process. If someone had been trying to pass us, we'd have been toast. But the speed Quinton was driving ruled that out. No one could keep up.

In those few seconds I thought it was all over. That I was going to die today, never live to see my brother I didn't know existed until a few days ago. We'd found each other on social media. I always checked for people with my last name, just in case I could find a connection to someone out there. Raised in foster care left me feeling abandoned by my own flesh and blood. I had discovered my parents were both dead along the way, within a few months of each other. But today I was going to meet the only family I had left I knew about. My first connection to real family. I was over the moon about it, but Quinton hated the idea. Said it was stupid to look back and let in anyone from the past, that I was only looking for trouble. It was all I could do to persuade him that I needed this. That if he'd do this for me, I would do whatever he wanted. The trade wasn't even most days, but I hung in there, certain my chance would come sooner or later.

"Sometimes he drives too fast. But so do lots of people."

"Is he remorseful when that happens?"

"Sure, he always feels bad after, apologizes by doing something nice for me."

"It could also be his way of manipulating you, trying to keep you from leaving him. It's called gaslighting, when he does it over and over again."

"We've established that I should leave him, okay! But I can't do that. I need a more permanent solution. What did you do, Sadie, to keep that guy from coming back and killing you?" I turned and stared at Sadie defiantly, looking at her until she finally met my eyes.

A buzz of electricity and the room charged with a different dynamic. I saw for a moment that she was considering spilling the truth, a look of indecision competing with her need for secrecy. To hide what she'd done. For fuck's sake, go ahead, tell me already!

"I didn't finish the test," Katie interrupted, her mood soured by the lack of control she was probably experiencing. Suck it up, Katie, and welcome to my world.

"I'm done with your stupid test. I need something concrete, okay, some way forward out of this nightmare. I need to know how Sadie escaped so I can too."

There, I'd said it. How long had it taken to get this far? Felt like days had passed while it probably had only been a couple of hours. Now we were getting somewhere though. Maybe this would all be over soon.

CHAPTER 21
KATIE

MONDAY 8:37 P.M.

"There's someone at the front door," I said.

Ashley groaned and took her face in her hands, rocking side to side, like this was the last straw for her. Poor kid, she had to be in an ocean of pain. I knew all too well what it felt to be adrift, unable to see the shoreline. After Brad and I split up, I'd spent months drifting around like a zombie, unable to focus on much of anything. I only came alive, and that was with anger, when he threatened to take Andy from me.

"It's Willow," Sadie said. Not unexpected, but still unnerving. "What do we do now?"

What now indeed.

Her innocent question sent me spiraling right back to the moment in the trailer with Merri, confronted by what I'd done to Wyatt. The dark blood pooling around his head in the hallway, his breathing harsh and raspy for a few minutes, then nothing. A deadly silence that stole all the breath from my body. I checked his pulse again and it struck me that it was too late to call for help.

"What did you do?" Merri demanded.

"I didn't know what else to do. He had a knife on you. He cut you, Merri, bad. Look." I pointed at her ankle where blood was dripping out and onto the floor. "We got to tie that up. You can't afford to lose blood, think of the baby."

I got to my feet and switched on the overhead light.

"Turn it off!"

I jumped but did as she asked. I scurried to the bathroom, grabbed a towel, and went back and wrapped it around her ankle, tying it tight as I could.

"We got to get you to the hospital."

"But what about Wyatt? He needs help too."

I shook my head. "It's too late for that. He's gone, Merri, he can never hurt you again."

"Dead?" My friend looked dazed now, like none of this was making any sense.

"We have to go. I'll call an ambulance." I pulled out my phone, ready to dial 911.

"No, they'll find him. Blame us."

"But you're hurt. We have to get help. It was self-defense." But a terrible sense of dread filled me. Would I go to jail for this? For protecting my best friend? He hadn't been actually attacking me, but her. A knife wound to the ankle is not the same as bashing someone with a sledgehammer. She was alive while Wyatt was dead.

"You know what happens to women that kill their violent spouses? No one believes them. They end up in jail or on death row. Remember the movie we watched about that woman called Sadie who killed her attacker? Burned him in his bed as he slept because he'd half-killed her, then promised to do the same to their kid. She went to death row for it before that group went to bat for her. Got her released."

"We don't have the death penalty in Canada."

"You know what I mean. Bad enough if I had killed him, but you did it. And a jury might not see it the way we do. What if you go to jail for years for this? You'd lose out on making something of your life. You want that to happen? No, this is all my fault. I can't let that happen to you. This world is stacked against women, and it only compounds if you're poor like we are. Nobody cares about us."

"What do you mean?" I had never seen this side of my friend before. I always thought I was the strong one, Merri leaning on me for things. She'd ask for my advice and usually acted on it. Now she was saying something I couldn't comprehend. Did she want us to cover up this crime? Was that what she was suggesting?

"We have to clean this up. Put him in the trunk of my car. Then drive him far, far away. Maybe to the river. Lots of people throw stuff into the Red River. That's a good way to hide bodies, right?"

"I guess. But you need medical help now. Your ankle's cut bad."

She waved me off. "It can wait. A couple of hours isn't going to change anything. You know how slow the ER is these days. Wait times are way up."

"I can't let you do that."

"Yes, you can. You know how often you've helped me. More times than I can count. I need to make this right. It's the only way I can live with myself. How could I explain to my daughter than I let my best friend go to jail for protecting me? Can't do it."

Too stunned by the events to protest, I focused

instead of how to go about what Merri was suggesting. Logistics were my strength, making a plan and sticking to it was my way of coping.

"We need to roll him up in something. A tarp or a large blanket, then drag him outside. I'll move your car closer to make that part easier," I said,

"How about the old wheelbarrow out back? We could tip it forward and hoist him in, then take him down the steps that way."

"It might work." Merri was firing on all cylinders, acting in a way I'd never in a million years could have imagined. Or seen coming.

Working on automatic pilot, we went about the job. I did most of the brute work, using a shovel to leverage the body into the wheelbarrow, bumping it down the three steps to the ground, pushing it across the grass to the old car and hoisting it in the trunk. There were no CCTV cameras in the area, everyone being too poor to worry about it, so that was a relief.

"Let's go." Merri was waiting in the front passenger seat after I had a good wash and changed into some clean clothes she scrounged up for me in her closet. She was so pale in the moonlight it was like looking at a spectral, and I worried that this had all been too much for her, though I knew I didn't look much better. I'd seen a stranger in the overhead mirror in the bathroom while I'd cleaned myself up. There was no going back from having killed someone. Just before. And after. My new reality was impossible to call. I had to live with this the rest of my life. And we could still get caught. It was more than an hour drive to the closet bend in the Red River, plenty of time for something bad to happen. Killing someone is the worst thing a human being can do, surely fate would make me pay many times over for it. Not that

I wouldn't have done it all over again. He had hurt Merri. Maybe not hit him so hard. But no going back. No do overs in real life. *Just keep moving forward.*

"Wow, that was close," Sadie said, jerking me back to the present by her exclamation of relief. "I wonder how he managed that? Willow's leaving."

"Thank the good lord," I let out a deep breath, watching Brad breathe on the sofa, his chest rising and falling, still sunk in what I hoped was sleep and not a coma. "Not sure I could stay hidden if anyone else was at risk." *At what point is the lifeboat sunk by too many clamoring aboard?* I'd always been intrigued by moral ambiguity, probably due to my knowledge of what I was capable of. What my friend was capable of thinking of and helped to carry out. But we both carried that guilt unlike psychopaths who had no conscience. Knowing that kept me somewhat sane. I took no pleasure from what had happened but only felt terrible remorse.

After we threw Wyatt's body in the river under cover of darkness and a sliver of new moon, we'd gone to the ER in Winnipeg as Casper's was closed due to a doctor shortage. Not certain anyone believed our crazy story of Merri stepping backward into the blade of an old scythe for cutting and stooking wheat left in the barn by her grandfather, but by then she was in labor. A terrible labor that racked her body with such pain I worried she might die.

When Josie finally made her appearance two days later, all wrinkled and blue, my friend was so exhausted she could only stare at her baby, a tear running down her wan cheek.

But the worst was yet to be. Was it karma? Were we being punished? It certainly seemed so when she died barely a day old. Would it have made a difference if I had gotten Merri to the emergency room sooner? The doctor in attendance said no, that the heart condition was too pronounced. But I was certain that what happened at the trailer and me allowing Merri to hold up getting medical treatment had brought on the pre-mature birth. If the baby had been more developed, maybe she would have had enough strength to fight long enough to have an essential operation? To get better. Now we'd never know.

It was a pain I'd carry to the grave. No making up for it, not in this lifetime. And Wyatt had to take on some of the guilt as well. Was he burning in hell for what he did that night? Striking out at the mother of his unborn child?

CHAPTER 22
ASHLEY

What else could I possibly do or say to get this pair on the right track to tell me what I needed to hear? They were so close to spilling it, I could taste the bitterness in my mouth. A sourness that made me want to throw up the little I'd consumed earlier.

"You were saying you've tried everything to get away from him before," Sadie said, absently rubbing the back of her leg. I'd noticed she did that a fair bit. Was it sore? Or something that bugged her because it was there. Must have been some bad cut when it first happened. I needed to ask her what happened. Maybe there was a clue there.

"Yes, I've done everything I could think of to get him to leave me alone the one time I left. Ran to a women's shelter, had an injunction against his approaching me in place, ghosted him on social media, nothing worked. He found me, broke down all my defenses, then told me if I ever tried that again, he'd hurt anyone who helped me."

"You have no family to help you? Haven't you made

contact with anyone since you aged out of foster care?" Sadie asked.

Better to lie now. It might speed things up. I shook my head. "There's nobody."

"I'm sorry. That must be so painful for you," Katie said, her expression one of sadness.

"Maybe one day someone will come looking for me. I was told by my social worker that my mom died while I was still in care. That she had no living relatives. So maybe that's why she couldn't look after me. She had no help. No one knows who my father is. He wasn't named on my birth certificate." Another little white lie. But who wanted to claim a man in prison for murder as their father? Anyone would have lied about it, I think.

"That could still happen. But a permanent address would help," Katie said. "Maybe no one knows where to find you?"

"Maybe. But it doesn't matter that much anymore. I've always been on my own, so I'm used to it." What more was it going to take for me to draw it out of them?

"If you're on your own anyway, maybe I do have a way for you to escape Quinton," Katie said, her eyes brightening at whatever idea she was going to suggest.

My heart thudded. Maybe this was it? "What? How? Please, you got to tell me. I need to know how you got Sadie away from the guy. Did you do something to him?"

"What? No, that's not important. What is important is I know someone who can help you change your name. With new documents, you can leave Winnipeg, go somewhere else, get a job and make a life for yourself. Start again. You have nobody looking for you now, so you could be safe that way. Save up for the birth of your baby. I can help. I've got some money stashed away. And

I can send you more for when you have to take time off after the birth."

"But I have no special skills. I'd make peanuts, minimum wage. Not enough to look after a baby on my own. And I'd be all alone looking after it. I feel like you both care for me, could help me out a bit as my friends, you know, with money and diapers and stuff. To just up and leave town means I wouldn't see either of you again, maybe for a long time. That would be so hard. Surely there's another way to get him to leave me alone? I don't think I'd have the courage to be all on my own. I'm not strong as you. Who was that guy, the one that was hurting Sadie?"

"What? Wyatt Draeger. Not important, only a guy from our hometown," Katie said. She looked stymied by my refusal to think her idea would be the one to fix the situation. Good. Now she was beginning to understand my predicament.

"So, is that how you fixed your problem, Sadie? You changed your name? So he couldn't find you?"

"It was part of it," Sadie said with a wince. She was hiding something. Something huge. My every instinct shouted at me that it was true making me want to press all the harder.

"What else did you do to protect yourself? Please, I need to know. Even if it's illegal, I'll do it if it gets him off my back." Would it be enough?

"You don't want to know, Ashley. Back away from the idea while there's still time. You get only one chance to live this life in the right way. The way that you can live with what you've done until the end. Some things— there's no coming back from. They'll haunt you till the end of days," Katie said, shaking her head ever so slowly

135

back and forth, as if the weight of the universe was keeping her from moving any quicker.

"I do want to know, no matter how bad it is or illegal. Here's the thing. I would do *anything* to protect my baby, anything at all. Hell, blow his brains out if I ever got the chance. He keeps his gun locked up for a reason. Maybe he knows not to trust me. I don't trust myself these days. Maybe it's the hormones? I don't know. But I feel things are coming to a head. Something bad's going to happen real soon if I don't do something to stop it."

The two women stared at me in disbelief. Had I gone too far? Given my hand away?

"Have you ever felt like that? That you had no other choice but to do something bad or wrong. You know, to make things work out for the better. And they did, right? Because you're both here now. So you had to have figured a way out. Maybe you could help me in the same way?"

Sadie and Katie shared a glance, then a slight nod. I froze. Afraid to move a muscle or blink. Was this the moment? The one that revealed everything.

"Will you tell her or me?" Katie asked.

"Go ahead," Sadie said, with a weary wave of her hand.

Katie flickered her glances between me and the monitor as she launched into her tale. "While we were still in high school, Sadie got pregnant. By her high school boyfriend."

"Wyatt Draeger," I said solemnly.

"Yes. He had a bad temper, always jealous of anyone that Sadie talked to."

"He must have had his good points too, right? Sadie was with him for a while."

"No one is all good or all bad, Ashley. It's a matter of

degree. It doesn't mean I ever trusted him or let my guard down around him. His dad is in prison for murder."

"Doesn't mean he's as bad as him. Maybe he wanted to be a better person than his dad?"

"Maybe. But it didn't go that way. You asked how Sadie got that bad cut on her ankle that left her with a permanent limp?"

"Yeah."

"He cut her there, deliberately, with a switchblade knife, two days before she gave birth prematurely to Josie from the shock and the pain. Said if he couldn't have her, no one would. It was to stop her from running away from him." Katie looked so bleak, so exhausted with the memory I almost relented. But I needed to know more. You have to wear your shit. Not like I hadn't. When I do something wrong, I try to fix it. Make things right.

"You were there, right? What did you do to stop him?"

"He was so angry, hauling my friend away in front of eyes. I was so scared. I didn't know what to do at first."

Sadie went and put her arms around Katie, her limp seeming more pronounced than earlier.

"But what did you do?" I pressed. The women both seemed lost in their mutual pain and memories now. Could they even hear me?

137

CHAPTER 23
KATIE

MONDAY 9:28 P.M.

I smiled at my best friend and patted her on the back like she had done for Ashley earlier in the evening when she'd been threatened by Quinton. Were we doing the right thing, confiding in a girl we barely knew? Making my best friend relive such a terrible time in her life just felt wrong. Like I was using her.

"I have an idea," I said. "It will be dark soon. Then we can get Ashley to safety. Take her to my sister Rose's place. No one would think to look for her there. Give us time to figure out the next step."

I turned to Ashley, certain this was the better plan, that I had finally figured a way out of this dilemma. That I now understood the young girl and her situation enough to help her do the right thing. "You can stay with my sister, Rose, and her family. She has room." Or more like make room, accommodations were tight in their mobile home. "Then you won't be alone. That's what you're most worried about, right? You can stay there until you have the baby. I can come and visit you. Casper is only a few hours away from Winnipeg. Quinton would have no idea where you are, he would *never* think to look for you there. You have no known connections to Casper, right?"

"I'm sorry. I'm confused. How can I possibly get to Casper tonight? Quinton's right outside. No way we can slip by him without him seeing me. He'd find me there anyway. No point in going there." Ashley looked more upset than anything, seeking to comprehend the logistics.

"There's another way out of here," I said, unable to keep the triumph from underlining my tone, unable to understand her reluctance when I had the answer. *This will work, it has to.* "There's a crawl space leading from this room out under the deck and into the backyard. Soon as it's dark, you can go with Sadie. I'll stay here. I have to make sure Brad will be okay." Without having to worry about Ashley or my best friend, I could confront Quinton. I had a gun. If he's as big a bully as I suspected, he'd turn tail and run if I confronted him armed. Then I could get medical help for Brad if he needs it.

"What? A crawl space?" She shuddered with obvious horror.

"It's the perfect solution, Ashley."

"But he could still find me, right?"

"We'll change your appearance. But the chances are slim to none. What's he going to do? Check out every small town and hamlet in Manitoba? I don't think so," I said.

"Is that what you did, Sadie? Ran away and changed your name and dyed your hair black? Is that all it took? You didn't do anything else to make sure that Wyatt guy left you alone forever? He's still out there looking for you?"

"You don't want to have to live with the guilt we live with every day. This will work, I promise you," I said.

"I don't know. He's so smart, he'd find me, I just know it." Ashley was back to biting her fingernails.

"I realize you're scared. That's okay. But this can work," Sadie backed up my plan.

"No. You're wrong." Ashley shook her head like she'd made up her mind.

Frustrated, I lashed out without thinking. "Doesn't keeping your baby safe matter more than anything? If you don't get away now, one of you will end up dead. Mark my words. You think I wanted to do what I did? Kill Wyatt Drager? There's no coming back from that. Once you cross that line, life is never the same."

"You killed the guy? How? When? Where?"

Ashley wanted details firing off the questions too quickly for me to answer, but I could barely hear her or concentrate, too shocked about what I had done. A loud roaring filled my ears, like a thousand angry bees were attacking my brain. The worst tinnitus attack ever. I couldn't believe that after all these years I had finally admitted it. Said that I had killed a man. A bad man, no doubt about it, but killing is killing. I hadn't planned to do it, to kill Wyatt, and it was in efforts to save my friend. But we'd covered up the crime rather than accepting whatever punishment would have come my way.

"The details don't matter, Ashley," Sadie said, giving the young girl a chastising glance. She pulled me toward her into a hug. I accepted the warmth her caring provided, trying to calm myself. I was shaking as I held back the tears. Too late for tears now. I was all cried out anyway, having shed so many tears over the years. I regretted telling the young girl immediately, not wanting anyone else to share my burden. But maybe it would be the thing to make her understand? A silver lining in an evil, black cloud that colored so many of my days. If I could save another person from the nightmare I'd gone through then maybe I could lay some of the guilt to rest. Maybe even forgive myself one day.

"No, I guess not. I have to pee bad," Ashley said. She hurried to the corner that housed the toilet and pulled back the curtain, vanishing from view. Nice of her to leave us alone for a minute, I thought absently, still hugging my best friend.

"You okay?" Sadie asked.

I tried for a smile but it fell lame. "This has night has been a living hell." I gave a rueful shake of my head. "God, I hope it's over soon."

"Don't worry about that. It's all over now. Thanks for confessing to Wyatt Draeger's murder. Took you long enough." Ashley stood with a look I could only call gloating. I couldn't do anything but stare at her in disbelief.

141

The look on their faces was priceless, realizing they had been played. I tamped down a bit of discomfort at tricking Katie, at the hurt and disappointment in her face as she struggled to grasp what I was saying. She was trying to help me get away from Quinton. *As if!* But I had sensed Sadie's mistrust all along. She'd been right to mistrust me. My agenda had not aligned with theirs. I wanted justice for what they had done to my older brother, Wyatt Draeger. They'd murdered him before I got to spend time with him. If I had been there, in Casper where I belonged, if my mother had not given me up to the foster system because she couldn't cope, he'd still be alive. And I wouldn't be all alone in this world. They took all that away from me.

"What did you do, Ashley?" Sadie screamed. In a flurry she rushed at me, snatching my phone right out of my hands.

"Give that back!" I shouted.

Sadie threw the phone at Katie and grabbed me by the shoulders, shaking me. "What is your game?"

"The confession has already gone to the cloud. It's backed up so having the phone is no help to you." I spit the words in Sadie's face as she held on,to me, all semblance of this being anything but a con game long gone.

"You—you used my baby against me? Listened to how impossible my life became after my baby died. How I was unable to protect her. What kind of monster are you? Are you even pregnant? Was that all lies?"

"Why?" Katie slumped to the floor, her back against the wall, as if all the fight had gone out of her, still holding my phone. A tiny bit more guilt escaped. I tramped it down. Okay, she'd been nice to me, but that didn't change anything. She was a murderer. Or was that murderess? She deserved to be punished for killing my brother. "It's okay, Sadie, let her go."

Sadie did as she asked, but I could see in her eyes that sparked with anger that she'd liked to make me pay a whole lot more for what I had done and was going to do to her friend. To both of them. She'd aided in concealing the body. And where was he buried? That's what I wanted to know so I could give my only family a proper send-off. I'd gone into this thing pretty certain I had the right two women, though not one hundred percent. But sifting through things, I kept coming to the same conclusion. Wyatt vanished just before the baby was born. Stood to reason his fiancé would know something about his disappearance. Had a hand in it. Snooping around Casper social media, I had gotten wind of rumors to that effect. Small-town gossips always knew what's going on. The pair had never been charged, there was no proof or body. But now I had a confession, surely the police would reopen the case?

"Because Wyatt was my brother. The big brother I

never got to have when my own mother gave me up to foster care. I was on my own out there. No one gave a shit about me. Then I found Wyatt, and I had hopes of being in a family for the first time. I was going to see him, he wanted to see me too, but you killed him a few days before I could even meet him. How could you do that to me? Take away my only living relative?" The memory of showing up in Casper nine years ago and discovering that Wyatt was missing had been a terrible blow. When he failed to meet me at the restaurant as planned, I had waited and waited until my ride had threatened to leave me behind if I didn't go with him right now. I'd had no choice but to go. But I promised myself I'd get to the bottom of things. I was certain he had not been dissing me. Not after having said how much he wanted to meet me. I believed him. And I began to research his life. It became my obsession, discovering what had happened to him.

"I didn't know. I'm so sorry, Ashley. I wish I could take it all back. I'd give anything for it not to have happened." Katie was as pale as the white wall behind her. Her eyes looked strained, her mouth slack, like she'd had the biggest shock of her life. She deserved that and more.

"It wasn't all your fault, Katie. Wyatt attacked me. He would have killed me if you hadn't done what you did." Sadie turned to me then, giving me a hard look. "What are *you* going to do now?"

"Send the confession to the cops. Soon as we get out of here. Quinton's not going to harm us. He was just pretending all that shit. He's okay. Not the love of my life or anything, but useful." I gave a shrug meaning *a gal's gotta do what she'd got to do.*

"He's not a good guy. Open your eyes. He drugged

her ex," Sadie said, pointing at Katie. "He's got you all twisted up, thinking you're not good enough, playing on you. All of that's still true. Unless you made everything up? Even the list? Are you that big a mastermind, that much of a gaslighting bitch?" She spit the words at me in complete disgust.

I didn't like the image her words were forming. I had good reasons for what I did and I wasn't going to be persuaded otherwise.

"No, you got this all wrong. I'm not like you. How else was I going to get you to confess to a terrible crime? You murdered him in cold blood!"

"Not in cold blood but in the heat of the moment when he was cutting a woman who was about to give birth to his child."

"Stop it! You're twisting things to your advantage. It doesn't change anything. Wyatt's still dead."

"So Quinton didn't threaten to kill you? You made up the whole story of abuse?" Sadie pressed.

"Not entirely. He does get mad on occasion. But I can handle him."

"Then you don't deserve our help."

"I didn't want it anyway!"

Katie finally seemed to come out of the slump she'd been in for the past few minutes. "Are you really okay, Ashley? Quinton's not the bad guy you been telling us?"

"Why do you care? I'm the one trying to ruin your life. Are you crazy or still trying to play me?"

"No one's trying to play you. You've done enough of that for all of us," Sadie said and went to sit by Katie, presumably to comfort her.

This huge victory wasn't making me feel quite as elated as I'd hoped.

"Are you pregnant?" Sadie asked again, her gaze making me uncomfortable.

I pushed out my chin. "Why do you care?"

"Contrary to what you think, we do care, about you, and especially about the baby," Katie said in a weary tone of voice. "The deal still stands, Ashley. If you need to get away from Quinton, we will help you."

Sadie looked less convinced; her lips downturned in that sour way she had.

But Katie's words confused me. "You're not going to fool me into letting this go, you know, no matter how much you manufacture sympathy for my situation."

"One thing doesn't cancel the other. I'm still on the hook but I will help you get away from Quinton if that's what you want, in spite of what you think of us. You need a friend, Ashley, more than you are aware. But just so you know, a confession is generally not enough for conviction. Especially if it's not accompanied by a body or some other evidence, especially DNA. The police already looked into our whereabouts that night and we were both cleared. It's been a cold case for a while. We could say that you forced us into saying what we did. And if Quinton was making you do it, that would keep you out of jail over what he's done to Brad."

I hadn't given that much thought and I didn't like the tables turning on me. Shit, she was right though. I looked to be an accomplice with Quinton if he wasn't abusing me. I needed to find another avenue of attack, a way to keep the spotlight off me.

"How did you explain the cut on her leg?" I asked, pointing at Sadie.

"Why should we tell you anything more? You'll just use it against us," Sadie countered.

I gave that a moment of thought. I did want to know

more, which meant I had to get this pair to trust me again. "Okay, you're not being recorded now, so it won't hold up anyway, right, in court?"

"Don't tell her another thing, Katie." Sadie said, crossing her arms over her chest.

"There's only one thing I want to know—where's Wyatt? I want to see him buried properly. You owe me that much at least," I said, unable to keep the tears from escaping and rolling down my cheeks. I angrily brushed them away. What did they care about him? In their eyes, he was a piece of trash. Just like me.

CHAPTER 25
KATIE

MONDAY 10:55 P.M.

"We don't know where Wyatt is," I said. That was the truth of it. The Red River had washed our sins clean in the many years and seasons since.

"You must have some idea where you dumped him?" Ashley looked frustrated at my answer. Was she being abused and in denial beneath that game she was playing with us? Much as I wanted to blame her, I did understand why she had done it. Not the way I would ever go about it, but then I'm not in her shoes. *Never judge another until you have walked in their shoes.* Pearls of wisdom from my grandmother. Where had compassion gone in our society? The patience and tolerance to listen to another's point of view? My grandmother, bless her heart, had a huge capacity for understanding. For dealing with people that went so much further than mine.

Sadie and I both shook our heads. "He's long gone. Maybe you can put up a grave marker one day or have a memorial celebration? Let loose balloons with slips of paper inside expressing good wishes or place flowers on a lake or river?"

"What river?" Her eyes bore into mine as she leaped on my words. "Did you throw him into the Red River?"

How had she zeroed in on that so quickly? Had she heard the same newscast I had earlier today? I gave a side glance at Sadie who sat very still tight to my shoulder. What was she thinking? I felt for her. All I had done on the anniversary of her daughter's death was make it the worst ever. Why did I have to drag up all this shit in hopes that it would help Ashley? Now we were being threatened by the very person we sought to aid. I understood the saying, *no good deed goes unpunished*, better than I had in my entire lifetime and wished I didn't. My faith in people had taken a direct hit.

"I heard they were dragging the Red again, looking for bodies. Maybe your crime is about to be revealed anyway? The confession might just be icing on the cake," Ashley said, her expression tight and mocking.

I glanced over at Andy resting his head on a pillow in the bottom bunk bed, wishing I could sleep as peacefully. If only I could roll back this day. But what really, even with twenty-twenty hindsight could I have done differently if given the opportunity? I couldn't stand by and see another woman abused because counterpoint to what Ashley was saying now, I was still convinced she was being abused by Quinton Riley. If it was within my capacity to help her, I would. I couldn't change the past. And I certainly couldn't bring Wyatt back or forgive myself any time soon for what I had done, but I could still help her. Make the pain of this day count for something.

"I'm sorry to have to say this, to be the bearer of more

bad news, but the chance of there being any evidence left is slim to none," I said with a grimace. Wyatt's bones would have been scattered long ago by the current of the mighty Red River. There was nothing left of him to find. Terrible as it was to admit, there was no way to correct it now. We should've been focusing on the present, not be dwelling on the past. But Ashley hadn't had the years since his death to process it, not like Sadie and me.

But it was time to ask the hard questions. Help her see things from a different perspective than she had lost a brother she never got to know. Yes, he was her last family, but that didn't mean she couldn't go on to have her own in peace and safety. She needed guidance more now than ever. "What would you have done, Ashley, if your best friend was the one being attacked by a man? Would you have let him have a go at her? Stepped aside and let him kill her, pregnant and defenseless?"

"I don't know for certain what happened. I only have your word for it."

"Why would I lie about it? How else do you think Sadie was left with a permanent limp? What have we got to gain?"

"You can go to the police and convince them of your guilt. That would work. You need to pay for what you did to my brother." Ashley's face became more animated, her eyes looking a bit off. My stomach wobbled, seeing the damage I'd done to her life.

"You don't think we've paid over and over for that terrible event, Ashley? There hasn't been a day gone by that I don't feel the weight of it," I said. "That I don't mourn for what might have been."

Suddenly Ashley was on the move, and before I could stop her, she had the Glock clutched in her hands. I had abandoned the deadly weapon on the bunk earlier when

I wanted to rush out and rescue Brad, making it all too easy for her. That was before I knew what this was all about. I was also having trouble processing things tonight, so much had happened, was happening in such a short time period, but I needed to get back on my game. Ashley was serious. And with the gun in her hand, she had just stepped up the danger.

Brad. Since the revelation, I had totally forgotten to check on him. I stared at the monitor, relieved to see his steady breathing. Then back at Ashley to realize she had been pushed too far. She looked like a woman on the edge of a precipice, far too pale with a crazed look in her eyes. I chastised myself for not locking the gun away earlier. If someone got hurt tonight, it would all be on my shoulders and I couldn't carry any more guilt. This was all my fault. There was only one thing to do.

CHAPTER 26
ASHLEY

I'm going to make them pay for their sins. For killing my big brother. They think they can weasel out from under it, make up for it somehow by helping me? Well, they have another thing coming.

The gun felt light in my hands. The adrenaline pumping through my system made the room turn snowy white for a moment before it corrected itself and I could see the pair of them huddled together still sitting on the floor. Then Katie got to her feet, shielding Sadie.

"You don't have to do this, Ashley. Give me the gun. Do you want your baby to grow up without a mother? You shoot one of us and you will land in jail."

"Who would know? If I shoot both of you and Quinton helps me cover up the crime? You said yourself that you'll never be convicted of killing Wyatt. Maybe we can throw the pair of you in the Red like you did to Wyatt."

"Have you forgotten it's being dragged again? It takes time for a body to break down. Months if not years."

"Well then, we can bury you. You got a big yard, all

fenced in. No one would know. Take you both out through the crawl space you mentioned. Where is it by the way?" Her eyes narrowed as she spoke, obviously considering her options.

"You don't want to live with the guilt, trust me, it will eat you alive," Katie said, her expression one of extreme sadness.

"Trust you! After what you did. Hardly."

Katie comes a step closer. "Stay back or I'll shoot."

"You're not going to do that. You're not a killer. You have to think of your baby. You want her growing up without you, in the foster system, with no family, nobody that cares like you would do? You have to be smart, Ashley. Think this thing through."

My baby girl. I imagined her growing up without her mother, like I did. The terrible pain it would cause her, scar her, knowing her own mother killed someone. Never getting to know the touch of her real mother. Even with just cause, she'd never understand my choice.

Katie reached out and took the gun from my trembling hands and I let her. I couldn't leave my child motherless. There was no one else to take her in. Out-of-home care was the perfect recipe for letting a child feel unloved, unwanted, and a loser. Her people would become the outcasts, the failures and the unwanted. Did I want that for her? Stopping her from caring about anything as I did for far too long? In the past hours I had gotten a glimpse of something more. A kinship I never knew existed. And as fragile as it was, it was more than I'd ever had until this moment.

"Now what?" I said wearily, slumping down on the bunk. I was shaking now, uncertain what the future would hold. What will Quinton do when he finally understands there's going to be no resolution to things.

Will he care? There's no money to be made in the house, not if what Katie says is true and the Warhol is a fake. He will care about that. His anger could be legendary.

"I want you to delete the voice recording you saved to the cloud."

Her words surprised me and I looked up to see Katie was holding the gun and it was pointed straight at me.

"What are you doing?"

"I won't let you hurt Sadie by having the cops reopen the investigation. And who knows what they find this time? No, I'm not taking any chances. I want that recording deleted and I want it done now." Katie waved the gun at me, underlining her words. Just when I thought they cared about me. Now they were using me for their own ends. The sense of betrayal cut deep, but I pulled on the old mantle of hardness I needed to hide how I felt. *Wait for the right opportunity to fix this.* I soothed myself with the thought.

"It's okay, Katie. I can handle it," Sadie says, her voice too high-pitched, suggesting she really doesn't believe what she's saying.

"Fine. I'll do it. Give me the damn phone."

Sadie got up and retrieved it for me, handing it over. I gamely went about doing what Katie was demanding, then showed her the screen as I deleted the entire confession. "There. You happy?"

"I won't be happy until I see you safe as well," Katie said, still holding the gun. "I want the pair of you to stay here, locked inside. I'm going to have a talk with Quinton Riley right now."

"What? That's not a good idea. One of you is going to get hurt. Quinton's not a man to confront. He will shoot you, Katie. Don't do it." Yeah, she wanted me to be safe.

Right. This from the woman who had pointed a gun at me.

"I have to try. I owe you that. Lock this door soon as I leave. And look after Andy, please."

Shocked that she was actually going to go after Quinton, I watched Katie quickly unbolt the door, then slip outside before closing it. Sadie scrambled to relock it but I got there first and pushed it open again. Then I rushed through the doorway, unable to wait.

I had to be there for this. I needed to warn Quinton.

CHAPTER 27
KATIE

MONDAY 11:19 P.M.

What was I doing? Confronting Quinton Riley could very well have been the end of me. But it was all I have to offer Ashley. She wouldn't see reason and go with Sadie to my sister's. Somehow, I had to show her that Quinton is a bad guy. He drugged Brad, and he would likely shoot me. But better that than having Ashley go back to him. If she could see what was going to happen on camera from the safe room, then maybe she would go with Sadie. It was the only hope I had left now. My friend knew where the crawl space started, the entry hidden under the supply box. She could lead Ashley to safety. Under it all a small voice was saying that this is the only way I can alleviate some of the guilt I have been carrying over killing Wyatt. That helping his sister would make amends for the grief and the need for revenge Ashley's been carrying around for years as well.

But as I came around the corner, gun in hand, I found Quinton standing in the middle of my living room with an expression of total anger darkening his face. And Ashley was suddenly right there at my shoulder, scaring the bejesus out of me.

"I told you to stay safe. Why are you even here?" I demanded, unable to spare a glance to look at her as I had to keep a sharp eye on her abuser.

She tossed the phone at Quinton, her shoulders straight with conviction. "I have the confession. She admitted to killing Wyatt."

"You said you deleted it," I said, confused.

Ashley shrugged. "I lied. There's another place I stored it. My email."

"Give me that phone," I said, gesturing with the gun at Quinton. I still had to protect Sadie's interest. She deserved none of this and I refused to have the cops questioning her again. She was in a bad place as it was. Reliving the nightmare one more time could have been her undoing. She'd spiraled into loops of depression that seemed to get deeper and wider with each episode and my heart ached for her ceaseless pain.

"Come over here," Quinton said with a nod at Ashley.

She did as he asked. Then he shoved the gun into her belly.

Oh my god.

What's he going to do? My heart raced painfully in my chest, my mind skittering out of control.

"We're leaving now. If you try to follow us, I will shoot her." He still held the gun pressed tight to her stomach. The sight terrified me to no end. Ashley's and the baby's very lives were in mortal danger. What could I do? The bastard has a tight grip on her, both physically and mentally. Nothing I said had worked. Now wasn't the time for more words, I was growing more certain by the second. It was the time to act.

Ashley had turned pale as a ghost, her expression one of pure terror. "What are you doing, Quinton? It's me. The mother of your baby."

"You don't think I know what you're playing at? You set me up. You knew all along the painting was a fake, right? Your stupid revenge plot didn't make us any money. Brad was kind enough to fill me in on that fact before he passed out. The divorce cost her everything. This place is a bust. We're leaving town right after I take care of Daniel and this mess you made."

"You realize he's going to kill all of us, right, Ashley? We know what he looks like," I pleaded for her to open her eyes, before it was too late. Time had run out.

"No, Quinton wouldn't do that. He's nothing like you. Right, Top Dog?"

The name Top Dog made me want to puke right then and there. But I held on to myself, fighting to find a way for this to work out, to have nobody die this day, slim as the chance seemed at the moment. I would sacrifice myself to save Ashley and her baby if it came to it.

Quinton ignored her question. "Stay back. Drop the gun or I shoot now."

"I can't let you do that," I said. He wouldn't listen to reason. He intended to do Daniel harm as well; I had no doubts about it. We were all dead if I didn't stop this right now.

I still had the gun in my hand. It was the only way as hard as it was to imagine. And without thinking it any further, I knew I would have to pull the trigger, aim it at the monster that was going to kill everyone if I didn't find the courage. I was a good shot so I knew I wouldn't hit Ashley. But I had to pray he didn't shoot her. It was a chance I would have to take. *Forgive me.*

But first I needed to get him talking. A split second of inattention is all I required.

"Did you make her write that horrible list, Top Dog?" I asked. Though the name made me want to puke, it gave him what he wanted and maybe I would get what I needed. *Direct that anger at me, asshole.*

"She wrote the damn list all on by her lonesome. She didn't need me to know she needed self-improvement."

"But you liked it, right? Her doing your bidding? Is this all a game to you? Do you enjoy intimidating women, Quinton? Is that what this is all about? Only way you can be with a woman is to bully her? Can't get a woman without abusing her?"

"Why you—"

I saw the split second he removed the gun from Ashley's belly to point it at me. I pulled the trigger first, a heartbeat before he could.

Quinton fell to the floor. Ashley screamed and slumped down at his side.

I rushed over to kick the gun away but she grabbed at it first.

"I'm going to kill you," she shouted, holding the gun pointed right at my face, tears streaming down her cheeks.

"Go ahead, shoot me. But I did what I had to do. He was going to cut ties with anyone who could incriminate him in the crime. Do you think he could have held a gun to your belly, right next to your baby, if he wasn't thinking of using it?"

Quinton moaned and grabbed weakly at Ashley, and the gun she was holding went off. Sudden pain erupted in my side and I stumbled sideways onto the rug.

Ashley looked with horror at the smoking gun. She dropped the weapon to the floor.

Quinton was quiet now. I crawled over to check his pulse. There was blood all around him from where I hit him in the neck. He was bleeding out. Fast. Ashley was in a state of shock and just sat and stared at nothing, her eyes unfocused. In less than a minute Quinton Riley was dead.

I pulled up my blouse and realized with relief that the bullet cut a deep path along my torso and wasn't lodged inside me, though bright red blood was streaming down my side. My skin was on fire but I would live. That thought alone kept me focused.

"Oh my, what happened?" Sadie asked, coming into the room.

"I shot him because he was threatening to kill us all. He had Ashley with a gun pointed at her belly. *At her belly*," I said it twice in disbelief.

"Are you okay, Katie?" Sadie asked, rushing over, obviously noticing I was bleeding through my top.

"The bullet didn't penetrate. I'll be fine. I just need to disinfect and wrap up the wound."

"I'll get the medical kit from the safe room." Sadie rushed away again. Andy came into the room and made a beeline straight for me.

"I'm okay, boy," I said, ruffling his silky fur. He licked my face, giving me some comfort. I glanced over at Brad, but he appeared to be still well out of things, his eyes closed. Thank goodness for small favors. He'd wake up none the wiser about this terrible night.

"What are we going to do?" Ashley asked.

Where to start? My mind was hazy and I shook off the inertia the last few minutes had caused. We were not out of the woods yet. It would be hours before this night was over. "We've got to rescue Daniel. Where is he?"

She gulped, hesitating to answer me, keeping her eyes averted.

"*Where*, Ashley?"

"He's tied up in the basement, okay?"

"Was that your doing? Or his?" I gave a nod in Quinton's direction. There was going to be a lot of blood to clean up. The situation was all too familiar.

Some color returned to Ashley's face. "Both of us had a hand in it."

"You know we're even now, right?" I said, watching for her reaction. This was still a fluid situation and the outcome still in doubt.

"What do you mean? None of this changes what you did to my brother or to Quinton."

"*You* shot me, Ashley, have you forgotten that? You helped kidnap and tie up Daniel and then assisted Quinton in robbing my home, even acted as an early lookout, coming over with that apple pie, right? The only way this works is if we all stay quiet. Do you want your baby born in jail? Or to have your daughter raised in foster care like you were?" I didn't enjoy pointing out the obvious, but she had to face facts. It was the only hope for all of us. Stick together. It had worked before; it would work again.

"That was an accident. I didn't mean to shoot you."

"You held a gun on me." I hated pressing her so hard but time was not on our side. We had to come up with a plan. Right now. "Our best bet is to cover all this up." But Daniel was the wild card in all this. How to keep him from going to the cops? I couldn't see any way to make that happen. The Daniel I knew would demand justice.

Sadie came back with the first aid kit, her expression so concerned I was more worried about her than me.

"Let's get you fixed up," Sadie said. She snapped open

the plastic lid, and began pulling out the medical supplies.

The antiseptic stung and I let out a groan of pain when she dabbed it on with a cotton ball. "Sorry. At least it's not bleeding too badly now. I'll put a large bandage on it over some cotton gauze."

"Thanks."

She finished fixing me up and pulled down my shit. Then looked me in the eyes. "What are we going to do?"

"I explained to Ashley we can't go to the police, or she goes to jail pregnant. I can't have that happening."

"I know. What can I do to help?"

I swallowed the strong feelings that rose up in my chest at her obvious determination to be there for me, no questions asked. Our bond really was too strong to be broken.

"You're the best friend I've ever had, Sadie, you know that, right?"

We touched foreheads for a moment before moving away.

I took a deep breath. "Okay. We need to plan this out. We can deal with Quinton. Our problem lies with Daniel Johnson and what he'll do."

"What about Daniel?" Sadie asked. She hadn't been around to learn what Ashley had told me, too busy looking for the first aid kit.

"He's tied up across the street, in the basement Ashley says. We let him go and he's going to call the cops immediately."

"Then we delay. We take care of Quinton first. Don't let Daniel free until everything's squared away," Sadie said. Where was she finding the strength? All this had to be wreaking havoc on her. A living nightmare. But then she had helped me ten years ago as I had helped her. We just had to do it all one more time. Prayed we didn't get caught.

"That poor man has been tied up for a few days now." Guilt at leaving Daniel in the basement a little longer struck hard. But what other choice did we have?

"Okay, Daniel stays put for now. Has he seen your face, Ashley?" I asked.

"No. I wear a mask all the time around him. Quinton did to."

I nodded with approval, that was smart at least. "Good. I'll let him go once Ashley is safely at my sister Rose's. In the meantime, we got a big mess to clean up."

CHAPTER 28
ASHLEY

I felt nothing, numb, like my body wasn't attached to my brain anymore. Quinton, the father of my baby, was dead. I couldn't bring myself to reach over and close his eyes. Instead, they stared up at me, accusing me of terrible things.

I lay a protective hand over my belly, trying to reconnect with myself, with my baby. *I'm sorry, little one. You were almost harmed by your own father.*

"Are you okay, Ashley?" Katie asked.

"I can never tell her about her dad. What he almost did," I whispered, my thoughts a jumbled mess, trying to make sense of the past few minutes.

"Your daughter doesn't need to know. At least now she stands a chance at growing up okay," Katie said, the smile she was going for falling flat. We were all under such strain. Nothing made sense anymore.

"We're all in this together, you know that, right? We only wanted to make sure that your baby is going to be born safely. Soon as we're done here, I'll drive you to Katie's sister's place," Sadie said.

I nodded. Yes, Katie did say she would help me, even after she found out I was trying to trick her into making a confession. Well, that wasn't a trick. I needed the truth. To know about what happened to my brother. How had it all gone so wrong? Now Quinton was dead too.

"Wha...what's go...ing on? Where am I?" a male voice interrupted, slurring his words making us all freeze.

We stared at each other before Katie got up off the floor and went stumbling over to the sofa where her ex lay prone under a handmade cover.

"It's okay, Brad, you're fine," she said, sitting down beside him in efforts to keep him quiet. Crap. Last thing we needed was for that guy to start causing trouble.

"Maybe we should take him to the bedroom?" Sadie said, moving to stand near Katie.

"I think we should. Could you give me a hand?"

I watched the pair of them work together to get the average-sized man to his feet and then the pair of them struggled off, his arms around their shoulders, leading him out of the living room and down the hallway. His head lolled sideways, his expression bewildered and unfocused as he shambled along like a zombie in a living dead movie. I knew how he felt. I had never in my wildest dreams of plotting revenge, seen it play out this way.

They were soon back, the strain showing on their faces. Katie swiped the perspiration off her forehead with the back of one hand. She was carrying a blanket and a plastic tarp under her arm.

"Okay, we need to wrap him up, clean the floor within an inch of its life, and bury him in the backyard. No point in the river, it's too dangerous right now with all that's going on with the dredging. I warn you. The soil back there is hard to dig, good old Manitoba gumbo.

Hard as cement after its baked under the summer sun. We'll all have to take turns digging and it's going to take most of the night."

"What are you going to tell Brad about why he's in the state he is?" Sadie asked, a worried look knitting her brows together. She chewed on her bottom lip.

"I don't know yet. He's a loose end. He might remember Quinton," Katie said, mirroring her friend's concerned expression. "Maybe I can say he was my jealous boyfriend I had just met? That he drugged Brad and I came home and caught him, then threw the guy out."

"But won't he want to report him to the police? You'll have to come up with a backstory that makes sense. And there's no one for the police to find. You'll have to come out with a fake name and where you guys met. Because all evidence of him is going to vanish. And with Daniel Johnson reporting a crime on the same day, it's going to look suspicious."

"I know! Damn it, it's getting so complicated. Okay, first things first. Let's get him wrapped up. There's duct tape in the second drawer down to the right next to the sink, Ashley. Could you get it, please?"

I gave myself a mental shake and got to my feet. Yes, follow the plan. One foot in front of the other until it's done.

In the kitchen I found the tape. I hurried to bring it back to Katie and Sadie. I couldn't look as the pair rolled Quinton over, placed the blanket and tarp under him, then moved him around until he was completely covered, using the tape to secure him in the cocoon.

Then it got easier, not being able to see him looking at me so accusingly with those open staring eyes. All three of us dragged him through the living room and into the safe room. He was awful heavy from working out. All muscle and steroids. And yet a woman with a gun had taken him down easily.

And then the doorbell rang.

CHAPTER 29
KATIE

TUESDAY 12:34 A.M.

"I'll get it," I said. "Wait here."

"Put something else on. You're covered in blood, Katie," Sadie warned.

I washed my hands with the bottled water. Then grabbed a sweater from the supply box.

"Better?" I asked, buttoning the garment up to my neck.

The doorbell rang again, like the caller was impatient.

Sadie gave me a look up and down. "You'll pass."

"I wonder who it is? Maybe it's the cops?" Ashley said, her eyes rounded with worry. Was she going to be okay? Worry about her state of mind surfaced. She'd looked defeated right after Quinton had died. "Maybe Daniel got loose? He did once before."

"I'll shut you in. That will keep you safe until I can get rid of whoever it is."

Please, please don't let it be the cops, I prayed as I made my way back into the living room. I threw the afghan that Brad had been covered in over the blood congealing on the floor, unable to stop a shudder at the gruesome sight. Did it smell bad in here too? I detected some pretty disgusting odors from having a dead body lying around in its own filth, having voided itself at the moment of death. I picked up a can of room deodorizer and gave a quick spray around, making myself sneeze in the process.

Another long ring of the doorbell. I had no choice but to unlock all three deadbolts and ease the door open. But just a crack. I didn't need any more company barging in tonight.

I gave a fake yawn, pretending I had been woken up and rubbed my eyes sleepily. Then I caught sight of who was waiting impatiently for me to appear. Willow. She was back and looked like she was prepared to demand answers. My mind scrambled to find them.

"I know Brad's here. His car's parked in the drive. I want to see him. *Now*, Katie. Go and tell him that I'm not leaving until I see that he's okay."

"Brad's fine. He's still sleeping it off in the guest room. He wouldn't appreciate your being here. He's embarrassed enough as it is. He got drunk last night, just so you know. Upset about my having Andy, I guess." A sense of pride that I had managed to come up with a logical answer gave my words a much-needed boost of confidence. But would it work to keep Willow off my back a while longer? That body needed to be planted in the ground as soon as possible. And every trace of what happened here tonight eradicated with extreme prejudice. A courage I only seemed to find when helping out a friend kept me upright, functioning well past what my body could endure otherwise.

The truth of it was I was terrified of being caught.

Sent to prison for life. Because as sure as the day is born, all the lies up till this point would come tumbling down if I didn't keep my finger in the dike. And I'd be charged with two accounts of murder. Most people when asked, probably would say they would help a friend hide a body even if it's only said in jest, but as my therapist likes to philosophize on occasion, sometimes a wide abyss separates theory and reality. I had crossed that chasm one more time and even if I felt I had no other choice, it was the toughest thing I've done. Harder than the first because back then I didn't realize the terrible burdens that come with it. Trust me, if you don't ever have to help bury a body for a friend in your lifetime, count yourself lucky.

Even now my moral compass was spinning out of control, no longer pointing True North as everyone likes to scream out in Winnipeg at the Jets hockey games during the singing of Oh Canada. I needed to stop that wild swing, get my actions more in alignment with who I think I am. But then maybe I've never been who I think I am? The thought scared me through and through. I had to suppress this, being on edge like this was a luxury I couldn't afford. Leave the moralizing until the deed was done.

I forced myself to focus on Willow who looked less certain now, her lushly colored mouth pursed into a pout. As usual she looked perfect, her dark curls all in place. I could only imagine how I appeared. How I smelled. Exhausted from the strain of all that had gone on since eight o'clock this morning, too many hours ago to count. But maybe that would help my case? Who'd believe Brad would have an interest in such a wreck of a woman, if indeed jealousy was her reason for barging in here?

"You got nothing to worry about, okay? He was just upset about Andy and had a few too many. It happens. How about I get him to call you soon as he wakes up? He's probably not going to want you to see him in the state he's in. He threw up last night—a few times." I gave a wince of disgust. When had I become such a good liar? I was suddenly disgusted with myself. If it wouldn't implicate my best friend, I thought now would be the time I would just stop running. Confess. I was becoming too tired from all this. And yet there was still so much to do before I could call an end to this day. A grave to dig, a house to clean to eliminate all evidence, and somehow make it right with Brad and Daniel going forward. Right, and try to keep the cops away.

My exhaustion must have gotten through to Willow because she nodded and stepped back. "Tell Brad to call me when he wakes up and not a minute longer. We're supposed to be leaving on vacation later today. An Alaskan cruise we've been looking forward to for months."

"I'll do that." I shut the door fast before she changed her mind. Then reengaged all the security devices. Maybe it was time to reassess the number of locks on the front door. Seemed I was the one doing the murdering, not some imagined intruder. I might as well leave it wide open and put up a warning sign about the inhabitants that read enter at your own risk.

I chased away my weariness and headed for the kitchen for cleaning supplies. The living room had to be made spotless before Brad woke up with all his faculties and began to ask questions. I set to work with a bucket of hot soapy water laced with bleach and a scrub brush before remembering my friends were still in the safe room. Chastising myself for losing the thread, I lumbered to my feet and went to check on them.

"Who was it?" Sadie asked.

I wrinkled my nose at the thickened stench in the small room. "Willow. Don't worry, it's been taken care of. But we need to get the body out of here right now. It stinks to high heaven in here."

"Agreed." Sadie punctuated her remark by rubbing the scar on her ankle.

"You going to be okay?" Sadie's leg still bothered her when she overused it. Moving a dead body hadn't done it any good.

"I'm fine." What other choice was there?

When I pushed the supply box over a few feet to one side, a square-shaped hole cut into the floor was revealed about a meter square. Pulling on the embedded metal handle I yanked the trapdoor open, letting in the musty air from the dirt-packed underground passage that led into the backyard. It came out about behind the house, exiting under the deck, near a garden shed. We could leave the body there while we dug the hole.

"Okay, we need to tie a rope around him, then I'll go down first, and you can lower him down to me."

I lowered myself down into the shallow space over a three feet deep and waited for the pair of them to push the body to the edge of the hole and then finally over the edge. It didn't exactly go as planned and the body ended up falling onto the earthen floor with a loud thump. He'd proved too heavy for much maneuvering, but at least he was safely underground. Between the three of us, we dragged, grunted, and sweated our way the few meters to the exit under the deck. I went first, pulling the body from the front while the pair of them pushed from behind. The space was too cramped for what we were doing, making the job tougher. But then was disposing of a body supposed to be easy?

When I hit the exit, I turned and unlatched the wooden door, kicking it open. The crawl space might have been shallow, but it was wide enough for some maneuvering.

"We'll get him out, then leave him under the deck and dig a hole first inside the shed."

At least all the activity was keeping my mind and body occupied. The mental torment would wait and be far worse, pounce under cover of darkness at some point in the future. As long as I could put that off, the better.

I led the pair into the shed to show them where we would be digging.

"The shed only has a wooden floor. It will be easy to bust through." I saw the idea taking form as I said it. "Then I'll cement the floor and no one will be the wiser." I needed to buy the quick-drying kind ASAP. Just not near home, but in a store clear across the city. Or better yet, buy two bags and use some to create another garden feature. Maybe a surround for underneath the bird bath and feeders to make sweeping up the seed easier. The practicality of the plan made me wonder further about myself. How had I become so capable of dealing with things that would make most people run screaming into the woods?

Every second I felt the weight of someone's eyes in the darkness. Watching. Judging. I shook off the guilty sensation. Time enough for guilt later.

"I'm going back inside to clean the living room. I'll put everything into garbage bags and dispose of them later. You two can start digging." I wanted Sadie to keep careful tabs on Ashley. I shared a meaningful glance with her, hoping to make her understand. The third member of our trio didn't look good with her weepy downcast eyes, not that any of us did, but the last thing we needed was her breaking down and doing something rash, like running to the police.

CHAPTER 30
KATIE

TUESDAY 2:55 A.M.

The burn of thick bleach in my nostrils was marginally better than the stench of death. But I persevered and by three a.m. I had made a good job of destroying any evidence Quinton Riley had ever been in my house. Even the fake, damaged Warhol had been hidden away in a closet to be re-framed at some future date. We just might get away with this after all if we stuck together.

But when I made my way through the cramped crawl space again praying it would be my last time tonight to have to do that, I found the pair of them squabbling, facing off.

"I want him buried properly. Not thrown in the ground like a piece of garbage! My baby girl should be able to visit his grave and lay flowers. How am I supposed to tell her that he's buried here, in this dismal place? It's not right. I won't have it!"

"Hang on, we can fix this place up. Sort of like a shrine." I scrambled for ideas, fighting exhaustion so extreme even my ears ached and if the ringing in my head got any louder, I'd swear a jet had taken off close by and was busy breaking the sound barrier.

The two women stood blinking at me. I was dismayed that the hole they were meant to be digging was still shallow. There were hours of hard labor left.

"Why not make it like a mausoleum. Flowers can be added and any things that mattered to him. Or you. Would that work, Ashley?" Marking the grave went against my better judgment, but I needed to placate her. Lower the risk.

"You can never sell the place though. It's the only way to hide our secret," Sadie said.

I shook my head. "I'd never sell it. And if you wanted, in a few years we could move him to the location of your choice. What do you say? We good with that?"

"Okay, I guess that would work," Ashley said, helping me breathe easier.

"We need to speed up this digging. I'll take a turn. You two rest." Though my muscles ached from all the extensive cleaning in the living room, I set to work gamely, using the spade to remove shovelfuls of dense soil.

At four thirty, I called it quits, though the grave was only half a meter deep. It would have to do. "It's time to get Ashley out of here. It'll be light soon, and the fewer people that see her the better." I still hadn't called Rose to ask her for the huge favor of taking in Ashley. That would take some persuasion and I wasn't certain I was up for it, though it had to be done. Plus, it was too early. Waking her up would make the discussion of my needing a favor from her all that more difficult.

"Shall I drive her to Rose's now?" Sadie asked.

"No, I haven't had the chance to speak with her. But don't take her home. Stay in an out-of-the-way motel until I call you. Get cleaned up. I'll set things up in the morning with Rose."

"I have to go back and get my things," Ashley protested.

"Not a good idea. I'll bring them to you. I have to deal with Daniel anyway. Best if you're not seen again." Could I really pull this off? So many unknowns. My stomach clenched with worry.

We made our way back under the deck, bending over for the task. Would the ache ever leave my back? But more pressing things lurked than the physical. I had to pray no one watched us as we moved the body into the shed. Why hadn't I had it exit into the shed when I'd had the chance? When I had it built? No help for that now. We'd been exposed for a couple of minutes and we had to suck it up.

"Grab his feet, Sadie. Soon as he's in the hole, you can leave. It won't take me long to fill it back in."

Dirty and sweaty, I hugged Sadie, then Ashley. "Now slip away before Brad wakes up. I'll call you later and meet you at the motel."

I turned back to my task and began to wearily fill the hole with shovelfuls of earth.

"Shouldn't we say something?" Ashley asked.

My brain had about shut down in exhaustion, but the plaintive look on her face made me pause. I stopped working. "Yes, of course, what would you like to say, Ashley?"

"I don't know. But something…"

I shoved back my impatience, the ticking clock growing louder in my head. How much longer would Brad stay unconscious? If he woke up and stumbled out here, we had everything to lose.

"Will the Lord's Prayer do?" Sadie asked. "We could recite that together?"

Ashley nodded. *Thank you, Sadie.*

"Our Father, who art in heaven, hallowed be thy name. Thy kingdom come, thy will be done on earth as it is in heaven. Give us this day our daily bread, and forgive us our sins, as we forgive them that sin against us. And lead us not into temptation, but deliver us from evil, for thine is the kingdom, and the power, and the glory forever. Amen," Sadie said.

"Amen."

"Do you think I'll ever be forgiven?" Ashley asked, still looking reluctant to leave.

I struggled to think, to come up with some words of wisdom that would start helping Ashley put this night behind her. Well, not that I had done such a good job of it, but you do what you have to if you want to survive. But she needed a simple axiom to live by, and even if it was an old saying, it did hold the truth. *"What doesn't kill you makes you stronger.* My grandmother used to say that at lot. It's from a philosopher, Nietzsche. So if all this life is a test, if there's a higher power out there in charge of our destiny, than I think we passed it. We're here, aren't we? That alone makes us resilient enough to withstand whatever life throws at you. You can come out of this stronger, Ashley, if you put it in perspective. Get it behind you."

I didn't bother to mention what she had pulled on me and Sadie. We'd moved past recriminations. And not like she hadn't said anything I hadn't already accused myself of.

"You'll go on to have a beautiful baby daughter. What matters more than that?" And maybe with that focus, the one that Sadie never had, would be enough to make her life.

"Nothing, I guess. It's just I feel so empty. I'll never know where Wyatt is."

"That's a discussion for another time. Please, you have to go." I needed to hurry Ashley on her way. "Now!"

The pair had only left when a loud series of knocks on the outside of the shed door made me lurch. My pulse pounded even harder making me think this was it. I was going to be held accountable. That is if I didn't succumb to a full-blown heart attack first.

CHAPTER 31
KATIE

TUESDAY 4:13 A.M.

"You in there, Katie?" Brad called out from the other side of the shed door.

Did I dare answer? I looked down at the hole where a thin layer of dirt barely covered the wrapped body.

Brad knocked again. Then a bark from the direction of the crawl space brought me the sickened realization that Andy had followed me as well.

The doorknob rattled as he tried to come in. I threw a tarp over the shallow hole. What possible excuse could there be for doing this in the middle of the night? Why didn't life come with a manual?

Nothing to do but face this. I swept the hair back from my face, pasted a smile on, and unlocked the shed door, cracking it open a few inches.

"What are you doing in there?" Brad looked grumpy as hell and none too steady on his feet.

"I wanted to get an early start on cementing around the bird feeder." *Lame, Katie, very lame.*

He looked affronted at my explanation but didn't call me on it. "Is Andy with you?"

"He's in the crawl space."

"What's he doing there? He could hurt himself. I knew he shouldn't be with you, and I was right." His outraged expression turned my stomach raw. What if I lost Andy all over again? *Please, please, stay where you are, Andy.*

"What are *you* doing here, Brad?" I turned the tables. I needed him to feel guilty.

"I came looking for you last night?" He rubbed his forehead, like he was trying to make sense of things. *Good luck with that.*

"I didn't even know you were here. Where were you?" I asked. "You shouldn't be here." I crossed my arms over my chest, giving him the evil eye. Oh, darn it, Willow already knows that I am aware of Brad being at my house. Well, brazen it out when the time comes.

"I slept in the guest room. I had a drink with some guy. Said he knew you, kept asking about the Warhol, next thing I was waking up alone. What's going on?" Brad swayed on his feet. At the moment I was grateful for his being drugged. The aftereffects of the hallucinogenic drug were keeping him confused enough to ease things a bit for me. I just needed him to leave. And most of all to not take Andy with him.

"I have no idea. What guy? Did you let some stranger into my house?" Denial, denial, denial works for political figures. Why not for me?

"What? No! You're crazy. Shit, and I'm supposed to go on vacation with Willow today. Our flight to Vancouver leaves in four hours."

"Then you'd better hop to it. Enjoy your vacation."

I waited for him to leave, then locked the shed behind

me. I slipped back under the deck to find Andy. He was busy sniffing the ground inside the crawl space.

"Okay, boy, we're going to make sure that he leaves before I let you out. You get that? I don't intend to abandon you, but I can't take chances. You understand?" I spoke to Andy as I closed the door to the crawl space behind me, then encouraged Andy to go back down to the safe room before Brad could come inside. I just made it, having heard his heavy footsteps in the hallway. I watched on camera as he stood at the door, knocking to come inside. No way. You can knock all day, but you're not getting Andy. Finally, he stepped back and with his shoulders slumped, walked back down the hall. I watched him look confused in the living room, his nostrils flaring. He was breathing in the fumes of the bleach I had liberally applied. *Please, go.* I willed him away with every fiber of my being.

Then with a final shake of his head, he left through the front door. Relieved, though he would certainly be back at some point with more questions. Crap. Should he even be driving? In all the kerfuffle, I had not thought of that. *Maybe I should go after him?*

I still had a lot of work to do before rescuing Daniel, but in good conscience, I couldn't let Brad get into an accident either. Not that I cared about him, but there were others on the road the bastard could hurt driving impaired. I raced back up the stairs and out the front door. Fortunately, he was still there, sitting in his car, the outline of his body visible from the streetlight gleaming on the pavement. He was still feeling shaky I imagined.

"Are you okay to drive?" I banged then mouthed through the driver's door window.

He lowered the window. "What?"

"I asked if you were okay to drive? Maybe you should

come in and have a coffee before you leave? You look like you got a terrible hangover."

He rubbed his forehead. "Yeah, maybe."

"I'll put the coffee on." Thought it was the last thing I wanted to be doing. I had so much to do as it was, needing to finish things and put other things in play. One thing I could do now though. I quickly sent another text to Daniel asking how he's doing? Later, after I was cleaned up, I would head across the street and use my key to get inside. My excuse would be I hadn't seen the pair housesitting for a while and needed to check on things to make sure everything was okay.

Brad trailed me to the kitchen and I set about making coffee.

"You don't look so good yourself. What have you been doing? You look like you need a shower. You got a spider's web stuck in your hair. And is that blood on your sweater?"

"Blood? No—yes, I did cut myself yesterday as it happens. Silly me, I was in too big a hurry to cut up some fruit for our girl's night and well, there you go." I brushed at my hair and turned my back to Brad to pull a mug out of the cupboard, quickly filling it with the dark brew. The intoxicating fragrance made my stomach clench with need. But I had too much to do to stop for the luxury of a caffeine fix.

"Aren't you having any?"

"Yes, of course." It would look more suspicious if I didn't. I added a dollop of cream and two teaspoons of sugar to a second mug, then filled it to the brim with the steaming beverage. A few sips of the stimulant and my brain felt less restricted. I stared and looked out at the yard through the sliding glass doors as I drank it. The pot lights illuminated the picnic table the three of us had sat at only hours before, getting to know each other. The sky was getting lighter even as I stood there thinking about how the three of us were locked together. Sisters bonded by fate.

"Katie. What happened last night?"

I whirled around. I had almost forgotten Brad was there, reliving events as I had been.

"What? I told you I don't know much more than you." I kept my game face on, unwilling to give anything away.

"I can't figure out why I can't remember what happened."

He sounded less sure of himself than I had seen him in a long time, if ever. Brad had always been the one to run things the way he wanted. But he'd rather walk away than bother to work things out, in truth. When I couldn't give him that, share all the events of my life with him, he taken it wrong and ended up having an affair before leaving me, calling me a cold, uncaring fish. Or at least a word that rhymes with fish. He thought I should be able to move on from my past and what better way than to share it with him? But I couldn't do that or it would expose Sadie. Catch twenty-two situations had been a staple of my life.

"You got drunk enough to black out, obviously. Are you feeling less shaky now?" Was my trial by fire over yet? I needed to get him out of here in the worst way.

"You got things to do. I can see that." His eyebrows rose in derision, the old Brad back. "Go ahead. I'm not stopping you."

Damn, could I trust leaving him alone? What if he figured more out? But how, the body was hidden though it needed better coverage and the living room was spotless. I didn't have precious time to waste arguing. I needed to finish in the shed and get cleaned up.

"I thought you and Willow were going on vacation? Don't you have to be somewhere?" He looked good enough to drive now, his eyes clearer.

"Yeah, good point. Thanks for the coffee."

He got to his feet. "I still got questions, Katie." He gave me a narrowed glance and exited the kitchen. Finally.

I raced back to the shed, desperate to finish one task at least. Scrambling inside and locking the door behind me, I quickly dug up spadefuls of soil and dumped them back in the hole, fueled by adrenaline and caffeine. Then after tramping hard on the soil with my sandals, I lay a tarp and tools over the area to help disguise the situation. Next, I needed to let Andy out to do his business before I showered.

Scurrying over to the deck and into the crawl space, I scrambled to the other end and exited into the safe room, intent on setting Andy free in the backyard. Instead, there was Brad fiddling with the camera system.

Oh. My. God.

He whirled around at my entrance, his expression one of horror. Andy lay snoozing in one corner of the room. I wished I was as oblivious to the situation. I glanced back at Brad as he now loomed over me, a confrontational expression marring his face.

"You were supposed to leave," I said, confronting him. "How did you get back in here?"

"You left the door unlocked as hard as that is to believe. What did you do, Katie?"

The accusation hung between us.

CHAPTER 32
KATIE

TUESDAY 5:37 A.M.

"It's not what it looks like," I said as the full realization hit me like I'd just been buried under an avalanche of thick white cloying snow that was keeping me locked in place, suffocating me. Another migraine loomed. Or was it the one continuing from yesterday?

"Is it supposed to look like you shot someone and then hid the crime? Because if so, then it is exactly what it looks like."

"I can explain. Give me a chance."

"You shot and killed a man."

"Did you not notice he was holding a gun to Ashley's belly, and she's pregnant? That he was intent on harming her? All of us?"

Brad shook his head. "This is something for the police to sort out."

He pulled out his phone and desperation built in me, thinking of what this would do to Sadie and Ashley. I couldn't have their involvement exposed. I needed to fix this and fast.

"What would it take for you not to call the police?"

His fingers stilled on the phone's home screen. I waited while he considered what I had said, each second an agony of worry.

His expression changed to one of greed.

"There is one thing I want more than anything."

"What? I'll do it. Tell me what you need."

"I want this house—this address. I want Riverbend. It's good for business. Living in Tuxedo on the riverfront brings prestige. I think I married you as much for this house as for what you were offering." A slight sneer of his lips made me want to strike him so badly I started to tremble with rage.

I couldn't believe what he was asking for. My home, my sanctuary. But what other choice did I have but to barter with the devil?

"You know what Riverbend means to me. How could you ask that of me? Do you hate me that much?"

Something flickered in his eyes, but he firmed his lips. "I don't hate you. I pity you, but I don't hate you."

"I don't need your pity! But I have nowhere else to go. Everything I have is tied up in Riverbend." Even my sanity.

"I'll give you a couple of months to find another place. You needn't move out tomorrow."

"Big of you." I glared at him. Once more a good deed on my part had brought about my downfall. And now I was about to lose Riverbend. I knew most people thought it was just property, that you take who you are to the next location, but for me it represented so much more than that. I had lovingly restored the older home to its former glory, until it shone with all the hard labor I had poured into it. I had planted beds of flowers in the backyard, created an oasis of nature right in the center of a big city. I'd hoped to raise my children here. I'd wanted a place for them to gather after school, to choose our home that they wanted to bring their friends to. Riverbend still waited for the pitter-patter of tiny feet, the laughter of children. And now I had to say goodbye to the dream if I was to keep my freedom. Save my friends. I had even hoped to bring Ashley and her baby back here when the heat died down.

"Fine. But I want Andy." The giving up Riverbend hurt more than I could say, but I prayed at least I could come away with my loyal companion. That at least Brad would allow me something to show for our doomed marriage.

He shrugged. "Deal. Never needed the hassle of a dog anyway. I just didn't want you to have him."

I was too angry to speak at his casually dropped bit of information, my thoughts shifting to how much I needed to protect my friends in all of this. If I was charged, the three of us would all do jail time. Especially if they looked into my and Sadie's past. What was to keep Ashley from spilling what she knew? In a moment of weakness, she could implicate both Sadie and me. I loved Riverbend, but I loved my friends more. And at least Andy and I could be together full time again. I might even go home to Casper. Rent a place for Ashley and me, maybe even Sadie would stay? The three of us bonding over Ashley's baby. No, that was too risky. Sadie would never go for it. And Ashley wasn't small-town girl material.

But it was time to leave the past where it belonged. Maybe it had been all a fantasy, thoughts of us all being supportive living together at Riverbend, but it was all I had. Something to fight for. My way of atoning for past sins by making sure my friends were going to be okay. I could help out Rose more. I definitely had to create a new app. Make some serious money to pay for college for nieces, nephews and Ashley's daughter. Maybe my own children one day. And now Brad has stripped it all away, leaving me with nothing but the sour taste of defeat.

"And while we're at it, I think some cash to sweeten the deal is in order," Brad said.

I stared at him in disbelief. "What? Let me get this straight, because I don't think I could be hearing this right. You want Riverbend *and* bribe money? That's insane. I don't have extra funds right now. I haven't been working since—well—you know. You cheated on me and we divorced because of it."

"Keep telling yourself that. I wouldn't have cheated if you weren't such a cold bitch to live with." He sneered. "Always shutting down whenever I wanted to communicate."

"Ever the charming gentleman. Ted Bundy would no doubt approve." My unexpected response made his eyes widen for a moment. He didn't like being lumped in with a known serial killer. But how could I have misread the signs so badly when we were dating? Thinking his charming ways endearing. Greed was what drove him. Nothing else, though maybe his libido had partially been at fault. The guy was nothing but a hound dog. "You already got the Warhol cash. How on earth could you be thinking you're deserving anything more? You're unbelievable, you know that." I shook my head in complete disgust. What had I ever seen in him? It defied common sense.

"At least I'm not a murderer."

"You can kill someone without taking an actual weapon to them. Destroy their lives for your own selfish reasons. I thought we were going to grow old together." Didn't he feel a modicum of guilt? And how was I ever going to forgive him for stealing my home out from under me? The one place on earth I felt safe.

"*Yada, yada.* Enough already. I'll expect the deed signed over to me when I get back from vacation. In the meantime, just think of all the incriminating evidence I've backed up to a safe location. That should keep you focused."

Too upset and angry to speak, I watched him saunter away. And at that moment the realization grew that I could not let him get away with this. He'd always be holding it over my head for as long as I lived. Demanding more and more money until I was bled dry. Then how could I help my friends and family. I had to do something. But what?

CHAPTER 33
ASHLEY

"What could be taking her so long?" I paced up and down the motel room, keeping a sharp eye out the window, chewing on my non-existent fingernails. The sun had been up for a while. Sadie was resting on one of the twin beds, dressed in the motel robe she'd begged from housekeeping when I had called dibs on the only one provided in the room. "Why hasn't she texted us?"

"She has a lot to do. She's probably dealing with the police and Daniel right about now. But don't worry. Katie can handle herself. She helped save me when she was barely eighteen. That says a lot about a person's character," Sadie said.

"Yeah, when the pair of you killed my brother." It still rankled and probably always would. But worse yet my baby's daddy was dead. Quinton hadn't always been nice to me, in fact he could be downright difficult, but in his own way he'd cared for me. Help me set up Katie when I demanded revenge. And now I'd never see him again. Impossible to imagine. I longed for him to take me in his arms and say it was going to be okay, he'd just been faking like he was going to shoot me. I was absolutely certain that was true. We'd been gaslighting Katie, wanting her to confess. Surely that was all part of it? I had been exaggerating his abuse. Sure, he could be mean on occasion, but he could also be sweet.

We were going to take the money from the haul and rent a place. Hide out until the baby was born. Now we're separated forever. It didn't compute. My brain refused to accept it. What did I have to look forward to? Meeting someone else to be the father of my baby? No man wants another man's castoff. I'd watched a Serengeti documentary that one time and even lions kill the young of another bloodline, so I didn't expect another man to raise Quinton's kid. I was all alone for the foreseeable future. The thought brings on more pain. A split-second mistake and my life's destroyed. How am I supposed to make it through this? It was all Katie's fault for killing my brother. If she hadn't done that my life would have turned out so different.

"You know he left us no choice, Ashley. Sometimes you have to do the unthinkable to survive. If it wasn't for Katie, I'd be dead." Sadie shrugged. "Some days I wish it were me that was taken instead. It's a terrible thing to live with, the death of your child who was never given the chance to live. Consider yourself lucky you're getting a second chance."

I tamped down the raw anger at her words, needing to focus on the baby. All that mattered was that she was born healthy and my getting upset wasn't helping. "Yeah, I know it could have been worse. But I don't think Quinton would have shot me. Katie could have just wounded him or something like that." *Why did she have to kill him?*

"You should try to sleep. It's not good for the baby to get upset or too tired. Are you taking prenatal vitamins?"

"No. I didn't know anything about doing that. I haven't seen a doctor. Just used a couple of those pregnancy tests." My ignorance might harm my baby. The thought hurt and I suddenly wanted to pick Sadie's brain for information.

"Soon as you're settled in Casper, you need to see about getting a doctor. The town has a fair-sized hospital because it services a couple of reserves. You should have no problem."

"Aren't you staying in Casper?" I didn't like the sound of this. Was she just going to drop me off like an unwanted burden with strangers, then ditch me? Of course I had only met the woman, but still, she was familiar while Katie's sister where I would be staying was not. Katie was okay when it came right down to it, she did think she was helping me misguided though it was, but that didn't mean her sibling would be nice to me. Plus, I understood she had children, so how much time would there be for me?

A bad case of nerves rattled the bars of my cage. I needed to get the hell out of here. Hold up somewhere. I eyed Sadie's keys laying on the dresser. The woman had a bad leg. She'd never be able to chase me. I could escape. Riverbend came to mind. It was a great house, pretty much a mansion, and what a lovely place it would be to raise a child. Katie was so lucky. I could see myself living there. How soon until it was safe to go back? I needed to talk to Katie about maybe doing that.

"No. Last place I want to be is Casper, Manitoba. Too many bad memories. I didn't go to the trouble of changing my name and appearance, just to go back. But you'll be fine. Rose will see that you're okay. She owes

Katie big time for always helping her out." She gave me a speculating look. "Aren't you sleepy? You should rest until Katie gets here."

"Maybe I could live in Riverbend? With Katie?"

Sadie stared at me. "There's going to be trouble over Daniel. He might recognize you even with a mask on. You know, body language and personal mannerisms. Your voice maybe? Too big a chance to take, at least for a while."

"But it could happen, right?" If I was being completely honest, as upset as I was about Quinton being dead, I still trusted Katie. I had felt safe at Riverbend for the first time in my life. I understood her attraction to the place. And being close to Quinton would be good. It was good she got it after the divorce. That Brad had to have been a fairly decent guy for a lawyer if he let her keep the house, though he did get another property and cash in trade. But I'd bet it wasn't as nice as Riverbend.

"Maybe, in a few months."

"Why don't you live with Katie?"

"I don't know." Sadie shrugged, her expression suggesting she was thinking about how to answer. "Not like she hasn't asked a number of times, in particular since the divorce. I guess it's because I don't want to impose. Bring my particular brand of sadness to live with her twenty-four seven. She's already in therapy. Same as me."

"Too much commiserating might lead to both of you more depressed?" I ventured.

Sadie's phone began ringing and we both stopped to stare at it. She grabbed it from beside her on the bed. "Katie?"

Dying to know what was being said, I moved in closer.

"Oh, no."

"What is it?" I asked.

Sadie shook her head. "I'm so sorry. Is there anything I can do?"

"What is it? What's wrong?"

Sadie set her phone down after what seemed forever, still looking stunned. "Brad saw the camera feed. He knows about the shootings. He's demanded the house in trade for his silence. And lots more money."

"That horrible bastard! We have to go back and help her." The implications hit me hard. All my dreams of all of us living at Riverbend imploded, gone up in smoke, destroyed by someone's greed. He already had a condo and that lake house. Why did he need to steal Katie's home too?

"No. She said to stay put. She's called the police and they're on the way. Now's not the time. She's not going to join us right away though." Sadie's expression shifted. My gut said she was hiding something from me.

"Why not?"

"Soon as she's helped Daniel, she intends to deal with Brad, try to talk some sense into him. But she'll join us soon. In a day or two."

"So we're just going to stay put and wait for Brad to come to his senses?" We should be helping her deal with Brad. I squinted my eyes, imaging pulling a gun on him and demanding he leave us alone. How dare he go after Riverbend! But after pulling the gun on him, threatening him, nothing else came to mind. Because threats weren't going to cut it, not if he had proof of the wrongdoing. In fact, him knowing about what had happened made him more dangerous to us than we were to him. If at some point, he decided that Katie wasn't paying him enough, would he go to the police? The life I was hoping to build for my baby sounded impossible as long as he was around.

"We can still go to Casper. She's told Rose that we're coming. It's okay with her."

"Nah. I'd rather wait for Katie. I wish there was something we could do about her ex."

"Maybe Katie can talk some sense into him. Maybe go viral again?" Sadie teased, but the idea didn't bring any gleam to her eyes. She just looked sad and disappointed for her friend.

"That won't help. He'll turn us all in to the police."

"I don't know what to tell you, Ashley. Brad is an unexpected complication and him knowing could ruin everything."

My anger dissolved and I slumped down on the bed, suddenly exhausted. I laid one hand over my tummy, wishing I had better news for my baby. I wanted to promise her a safe place to be born and raised.

"What's Rose's place like?"

"Erm, kind of small, I guess. A mobile home of some sort, I believe."

"So we're all packed in like animals while Brad and that Willow person gets the big, beautiful house. That sucks."

"Better than on the streets, Ashley. At least you'll be safe. And it won't be for long. I imagine that Katie will come up with something better soon."

"But how if that moron Brad intends to drain all her funds?" Brad loomed in my mind again, this time with a bullseye painted right between his stupid, greedy eyes. I always wanted to learn how to use a bow and arrow. What better time than the present?

"I don't know. But you should rest, sleep. Things have a way of working themselves out.

But do they really?

So far things had only been getting worse for me. I wanted to leave right now, but getting up again seemed a monumental task. If only I wasn't so tired. Well, the room was paid for, might as well stay for a few hours at least. Rest up for the sake of my baby, then decide what to do.

CHAPTER 34
KATIE

TUESDAY 7:17 A.M.

A long hot shower helped, washing the stench of death away, but exhaustion was claiming me. I'd been up for twenty-four hours straight, under the worst strain of my life, and the ordeal was not over yet. I looked at my bed with such longing, it brought tears to my eyes. Could I take just a short cat nap? No, it wasn't right. Poor Daniel was tied up across the street and needed my help. I still had to finish cementing over the hole in the shed. And deal with the Brad situation. The pair were flying out later today to Vancouver and catching the cruise ship. That left little time for me to plan.

Nurses and doctors in the ER worked overtime routinely during the pandemic, I should be able to manage a few more hours. Just keep moving and drinking coffee, Katie. Giving my bed one last look of longing, I headed to the kitchen to prepare a triple espresso, my only hope of keeping myself moving. Motivation, now that I had in spades.

I stared at the triple locks on the front door as I braced myself for going over to Daniel's. One time I forget to engage then and what happens? A monster comes in and tries to destroy my life. Because that was how I thought of Brad now. How I could ever have been taken in by him defied reason. I shook my head and ventured outside. It was a lovely cool summer morning before the intense heat of day arrived and I shivered a bit in my white cotton blouse and beige capri pants.

Dew was sparkling like a multitude of tiny diamond chips on the grass as I crossed the boulevard and into Daniel's front yard. Sweet birdsong filled my ears, and I was hard pressed to go inside, discover the horror within. The world had begun again for nature and everyone else in the freshness of a brand-new morning, but it would be destroyed soon enough. Bracing my myself, I unlocked the front door with the key that Daniel had given me years ago. One good thing, Daniel did not have CCTV installed.

"Anybody home?" I called out, needing to make it sound legit. "Daniel?" I tried a few more times as I moved through the main floor. I needed to find Ashley's stuff and hide it before finding Daniel in the basement, make sure there was nothing incriminating around. I found the backpack she had described as hers in one of the bedrooms and decided to tug it over my shoulders, knowing there was no other way to legitimately get it out of there. Then I headed to the stairs that led to the basement. *Please, please, be okay*, I prayed as I descended into the bowels of Daniel's house.

I took in the view. A pair of eyes stared at me from across the basement. A rag tied around his mouth, but I still recognized Daniel. He was alive and laying on the floor, his hands bound up. I had to make this look good, like I had no idea of what had transpired.

"Oh my goodness, Daniel! Are you okay?" I raced across the floor and kneeled down at his side, struggling to free the man. But he was chained up with no key in sight.

I managed to get the gag off, then untied his hands, waiting while Daniel took a couple of deep ragged breaths. His eyes looked sunk into his face, ringed with purple shadows. Guilt struck. While I had been showering in preparation for dealing with the police, he's been like this, unable to move or defend himself not knowing if his capturers were coming back. A large welt on the size of his forehead looked raw and painful. Someone had punched him. Probably that bully Quinton. Hard to feel any sympathy for the father of Ashley's child when he did things that defied human decency. What had Daniel done to him other than being in the wrong place at the wrong time? Knowing it was tied to my actions nine years ago didn't help with the guilt.

"Are you okay?" I asked, handing him a bottle of water.

He took the water and drank half of it, then swiped his hand over his mouth. "Better now. Are they gone?"

"Who?"

"The home invaders that tied me up. A man and a woman. Bloody hell. I was minding my own business and out of nowhere, bam, and I'm struck by the guy when I'm in my own garden."

"I'm calling the police." I pulled my cell phone from my pants pocket.

"Are you sure there're gone? They've been here for a few days. But I haven't seen them since yesterday around noontime judging by the light. Did you see anything?"

His glance darted about the room as if he expected to be assaulted at any moment.

I shook my head, wishing I could say more, that they would never be back to bother him. "Sorry, nothing."

"Then why are you here?"

"You weren't answering my calls or texts. I got worried and thought I'd better check." When had I become so good at lying? Truthfully, since I was eighteen. Nine long years of hiding the truth with no end in sight. And it was only going to get worse. "Did you get a good look at them?"

"No, they wore masks. But they were young, about your age, I think, by the way they moved. Not old and stiff like me."

"You're not old."

"I feel every day of my fifty-one years today, let me tell you."

I didn't argue any further, but dialed 911 and waited for the operator to answer before giving all the particulars.

"They're sending the police."

"Good. I want those bastards caught. I can only imagine the mess upstairs. Did they clean me out?"

"I don't think so. It's seemed okay except for some beer bottles and takeout bags in the living room. But I saw that your computer was in place and your TV, so I'm not certain what they were after." Damn, should have removed some of the valuables, otherwise it looked suspicious. Why would they be here if not to rob the joint? "Maybe they got spooked by something before they had a chance to steal anything?"

"Maybe?" He grimaced. "Could you give me a hand up?"

I helped him to his feet, letting him lean on me. The

chain on his ankle rattled, making me look frantically around for a key. Of course it wouldn't be here with him. It must be upstairs.

"I have to get that chain off."

He looked down at his leg as if he'd forgotten about being tied to the leg of the frig.

"I'll check upstairs for the key. Will you be all right alone for a few minutes?"

"Go, find the key. Or get a locksmith. Something, please."

"I'll pull a chair over and you can sit while you wait."

I tentatively let him go and hurried over to an old chrome chair leaning against a wall, dragging it over for Daniel to sit on. The steel-like legs squealed on the cement floor, making me cringe in discomfort.

"I'll be right back."

"And I'll be waiting right here." The bit of spunk in his tone lessened some of the guilt for leaving him tied up a moment longer than necessary and I took the stairs two at a time to the main floor. I needed to find that key.

Sirens alerted me to the police arriving any moment as I searched frantically around the house for the damn key. Where in the hell was it?

A loud knock on the front door. "Police. Open up."

Abandoning my search, I opened the door to two officers, one male and one female from the Winnipeg Police Service. The man had dark, closely cropped hair and a no nonsense look about him while the woman was a few years younger and sported a tidy mid-brown bun. She also had that wary-eyed look. I totally understood. The way things stood in this world, who knew who the enemy was? Nobody seemed to be who they said they were anymore. I had just been duped by Ashley to a certain extent, uncomfortable as the thought was.

"A crime was reported at this residence?" the female asked.

"Yes, I'm a neighbor—"

"Your name?" the male officer asked, pulling out a pad of paper.

"Katie Kelly. Daniel Johnson, the owner, is tied up in the basement. I was looking for the key to unlock the chain. But I can't seem to find it."

"Show us."

The three of us tramped through the house. The keys and items on the officers' belts clinked and rattled, making me more nervous, reminding me too much of a jail cell.

Calm down. I just needed to keep it together. Not like I had anything to do with this. Only thing I was guilty of was helping an abused woman escape. Well, that and killing her abuser.

My hands turned clammy from sweat. If they ever discovered what had happened across the street, I would spend the rest of my life in jail. The backpack began to itch the skin on my back, pressing into the damp of my blouse. I wanted nothing more than to take it off but that would have to wait.

"He's in the basement," I said, pointing at the open door in the kitchen.

"Show us the way, please," the woman said.

"Shouldn't I be looking for the key to unlock him?"

"First we need to assess the situation, then we'll get any tools required," the male officer said in an official tone. His unsmiling face wasn't settling any of the roiling nerves in my stomach.

I did as he asked, then stepped aside while a short discussion took place with Daniel. It was hard to concentrate on what they were saying, I had so much to go and do today. When were Brad and Willow leaving on their cruise? Was there time to make another plea for clemency? How were Sadie and Ashley doing at the motel? Or had they already headed for Casper? Rose hadn't been too keen on having company, complaining that the trailer was already crowded, but she'd relented and said she'd clear out one bedroom for the pair.

One of the officers was leaving and I blinked, wondering what had been decided. I couldn't exactly ask. It would make me look like a dolt, not capable of paying attention to a neighbor in need.

"Katie, Daniel said you tried to reach him which is why you came by today? You were concerned about him?" the female officer asked.

Nodding, I pulled out my phone as if proof was required.

She waved me off. "That's fine. Good thing you did check. Very neighborly of you. I wish more people cared about making sure things are okay for others in their neighborhood."

I felt the heat rise in my cheeks, knowing the officer's praise was unwarranted. I should have been here sooner.

"Did you see anything? Suspect anything out of the ordinary in the last few days?" she asked.

"No, sorry, nothing seemed different."

"You never saw the two people who squatted in this house for a few days?" Her eyebrows rose, her expression somewhat skeptical.

"Yeah, but only from a distance. I didn't meet them or anything." Oh god, what if someone saw something? Like Ashley coming over to my place? I should have thought of this, prepared myself better. Maybe I'm not so good at lying as I thought. The maybe if I wasn't exhausted from being up all night, I could do a better job of it. But I could hardly have a sleep to restore myself with Daniel in peril.

"You have CCTV on your property? Perhaps we can check it?"

"I'm sorry, I've been meaning to fix it. The software needs updating. It's not storing the feed at the moment."

She accepted my answer, but a brief look of annoyance crossed her face. The other officer came down the stairs just then, his boots thudding on each step.

"I've got some bolt cutters. We should have you free shortly, Mr. Johnson."

My cell phone rang and I excused myself to answer it.

"Katie! It's Rose. I have terrible news!"

"What's wrong?" My worried tone caused the two officers to give me a quizzical stare. Daniel was too busy to notice, rubbing his ankle where the chain had been cut off.

"A fire. The trailer—it's gone. Everything has burned. Everything! What are we going to do?"

Her horrifying news set my tired nerves to jangling.

CHAPTER 35
KATIE

TUESDAY 8:25 A.M.

Stunned at my sister's news that her home had burned to the ground; I could only stare at my phone in horror for a split second.

"Katie?"

"I everyone okay? No one got hurt?"

"No, we all got out. I don't have a clue how it started. Crap, we don't even have insurance. What am I going to do, Katie?"

The desperation in my suddenly homeless sister's voice pushed hard against my urgent need for rest. That would have to wait now. "Rose, don't worry. You can stay with me at Riverbend for as long as you need." How could this be happening now? And how could I have promised my sister something I couldn't provide, at least not long term? The clock was ticking down on me being forced to leave my home, let alone inviting more people to stay. But family's family, and nothing was going to get in my way of opening my home and my heart to my little sister. And most definitely not Brad.

"My sister's home just burned down. Thankfully everyone got out safely. Is there anything else, officers?"

"I'm sorry to hear that. Terrible thing." The woman shared a look with her partner. "If there's anything else, we've got your contact number."

"I don't think I can help much more. I didn't see anything."

"You never know. Sometimes things come back to witnesses once things calm down."

Yeah, right. I just wanted to slip right off their radar.

"Sorry, Daniel. I have to leave. My sister and her family are moving into Riverbend today. Do you need anything before I go?" I needed to call Sadie and Ashley and let them know the deal. And plead once more with Brad. Surely now that the situation had changed, his better self would kick in and I could keep the deed to a home I had paid for in thousands of hours hunched over my computer?

"No, thanks for all this. I was beginning to think I was a goner. If they hadn't come back or you hadn't thought to check on me..."

He left his words hanging and I gave him a hug of reassurance. "You'll be fine now. Maybe install some safety features? Keep your mind busy thinking about getting that done. I can help with recommendations."

Thankful to be escaping the disconcerting looks of the police, I hurried up the steps and out the front door. I had an urgent need to get to my sister to see for myself that she was okay, but I had something I had to do first. I called Sadie as I crossed the street, letting her know the situation. She promised to see to Andy while I was gone.

Back in the house, I quickly pulled some cold bottled

water from the refrigerator, packed a small bag, then grabbed my purse and car keys. Hardest thing was leaving Andy, but I couldn't very well take him where I was going.

I left Ashley's backpack for her on the coffee table in the living room. The scent of bleach still tainted the air, though it had eased somewhat. Walking into the garage, I decided to call Brad from the road on the hands-free device. Give him one last chance to see reason. Maybe things would work out after all? Yeah, right. With a dead body in the shed, incriminating evidence on file, oh, and now add lying to the police again.

With every second that passed, my worry grew. The short conversation with Brad did not go well. In fact, it had made the situation far worse. He refused to discuss it. Maybe he thought I'd record it? Incriminate him? Actually, that sounded like a fairly decent option. If I had something on him, maybe I could keep my home and provide security for a lot of people now depending on me. But what? Though he was blackmailing me, I looked like the bad one, not him. It was only my word against his.

So now I was racing to see him in person, a seething anger growing inside me at the unfairness of the situation for Brad was now insisting I had to be out by the time he returned from his vacation, that he didn't want my sister and her brood in Riverbend with the potential to downgrade the house. If there was such a thing as karma in this world, he'd never return from said vacation.

Sadie had been upset as well, to the point of saying we should bury him along with Quinton in the shed. I was grateful she didn't bring up my poor taste in men, but instead supported me a hundred percent. Sadie at least had a place to live, small and cramped as it was, barely big enough for her, let alone another person. She lived there to punish herself, I often thought. But it was no place for Ashley or the baby.

At the airport, I booked my flight to Vancouver and confirmed my reservations on the Alaska cruise line under a false name. I was too late to catch Brad at home, but not too late to confront him on vacation. He might think I was stalking him, but I liked to think it was to make him see sense. I needed his promise that he wouldn't take Riverbend from us. Maybe it was the exhaustion talking, maybe it was I'd just finally had enough, but I was not going to let this go.

CHAPTER 36
KATIE

TUESDAY 11:55 P.M.

I woke up groggy, hardly remembering boarding the plane or the ship. I'd been on autopilot ever since leaving Winnipeg. Guilt hit that I hadn't been at Riverbend to welcome Rose and her family, but I reminded myself what I was doing was far more important, ensuring we all had a sanctuary. I had no idea how these next few days were going to play out, but I needed to keep Brad in one spot, talk some damn sense into him. Make him let it go. I had a plan B that I prayed I would not need to resort to. But if he drove me to it, it would be on his head. A man that can blackmail a woman he was supposed to love and cherish, is not a man in my opinion.

After a quick shower, I headed out, needing to find out more about Brad's location. Fortunately, it was a small cruise ship so I would run into him and Willow soon I was quite certain. I knew him well enough to know he'd be up late celebrating a day of victory over his ex.

Dressing in a flowery sundress I had thought to pack so I would blend in with the tourists, I added a white cardigan and matching flats and headed for the casino, the place I was most likely to run into Brad. He loved to gamble. Sure, he'd be shocked to see me. But it would give me the advantage. I want him to see how far I was willing to go for my family. Strength I never knew I had led me to stride confidently along the corridors. I had a moment of wishing I had back up, a friend. But if things went south, at least my will leaves Riverbend to Rose and Sadie meaning Brad would never get his greedy hands on it.

The sounds of slot machines led the way into the gaming room. I stopped just inside the doorway to orient myself. A sudden loud noise of fanfare took my attention away from my search for my ex. Someone had won big. Lucky them.

I joined the crowd that surged over to the winner's spot like lemmings to the sea though that theory has been proved incorrect by scientists. Maybe people were more predictable than nature? I hung on the edge of the group and stared at the winner with disbelief.

Brad Kenneth Bennett, my despicable ex.

How could this be? Karma was kicking me right in the face. Of all the people who could use the money, the sneaky, double-crossing lawyer had to win?

Hanging back to watch, I viewed with narrowed eyes everyone being excited for the man who had just won nine hundred thousand dollars. Some people shook his hand or clapped him on the back, some grimaced then covered it up.

Then I had a new, far better thought. With him in

such a good mood, maybe this was the time to approach him? He certainly didn't need Riverbend now with nearly a million dollars in hand. That money would buy a down payment on any luxury home he wanted in Winnipeg. *But just not too close to Riverbend, please.*

"Congratulations, Brad," I said, striding up to him with a smile pasted on my lips once the crowd disbanded, looking for their own win.

It was his turn to look confused for a micro-second before he recovered his usual arrogant position.

"Katie. What are you doing here? I thought you had an emergency at home?"

"I needed some time out." I shrugged. "Thought maybe a cruise was in order. Seems to be working for you. Looks like you're all set up now. Wish I was so lucky. I could sure use the cash now that Rose, Joe, and her children are homeless."

He had the grace to turn redder under his tan. "Yeah, sorry about that. But you know what her kids are like. Always destroying something. You must know that one of them was probably involved with burning down their home in the first place, right?" His expression turned to one of disgust. "If you can call that tin shack a home. But I certainly can't take a chance they'll do that to Riverbend."

"They're just kids being kids. They don't plan to do harm, unlike grownups."

"So, you all alone?"

"Yeah." I looked around. "Where's Willow?"

"She had a headache and turned in early. Good thing I stayed, eh." His gloating mug was about all I could handle. Bile splashed the back of my throat and I fought against not upchucking on his expensive shoes. But I needed to have this discussion and feeling ill wasn't going to stop me.

"Could we have a drink? I'd like to talk a bit more."

He shrugged. "What's the point? I'm not changing my mind, if that's what you're after."

"So you'd put a family out on the street? What do you think the press will think of that?"

"Are you threatening me? I know what you did, Katie. Watch yourself." He strode away after blessing me with a dark look.

I stood there filled with defeat, my shoulders slumping. I tugged the sweater around myself, chilled from the air conditioning. The trip had been a waste of time, effort, and money. I should have been home right now helping Rose. Brad didn't need to know they were moving in until he came home. Maybe we could become squatters? Not likely, not with what he held over my head like a broad sword ready to separate my head from my body. My entire existence was on the line because of him. I'd never again be able to draw one easy breath knowing he could turn me in at any second to the police. That monster would be in control of my life forever. Whatever future money I made would be drained away by his greed. He was as bad as any pimp, but worse, because he'd never admit he was.

Leaving the casino, I found myself following Brad at a discrete distance. At least then I would know what cabin he and Willow were staying in. Brad was just begging for a plan B.

When he went inside, I lingered nearby being careful to stay out of sight. He might decide to head out again, especially if Willow wasn't up to celebrating. He could be a heavy drinker at times, staying up until all hours. After winning big, thinking he was getting Riverbend as well, he might leave the cabin again.

Maybe I needed to hire a private investigator to follow him? He must have had a skeleton in his closet somewhere I could bribe him with. If he could blackmail me, he must have done something similar in the past. He'd come back at me so quickly; it was like he was prepared to do the dirty at all times. The fact that I had fallen for such a man hurt more with each passing hour, each breath I sucked into my lungs.

My phone buzzed and I hesitated to answer it, not wanting to give my location away. But I swiped at the screen when I realized it was only a text, and the action caused the short message to be revealed. I had to read it three times to make certain I had read it correctly.

> Meet me on deck. I want to help.
> Sadie xx

Sadie, my friend, had followed me. And the best part, wanted to be here for me. My heart leaped with joy, the news providing a moment of such a sense of being cared about that it defied description. I wasn't alone, struggling against the current like a salmon going upriver to spawn, but a woman with a friend staunchly at her side through thick and thin. It doesn't get better than that. Somewhere along the way she must have forgiven me for being too late that day, for not stopping the tragedy.

I scurried away, arriving topside breathless with anticipation. The full moon shone down on the whitened decks, adding a surrealness to the atmosphere as I looked around frantically for my friend. There were few fellow passengers about, most likely in bed or in the casino. It wasn't a fully booked cruise which I was grateful for, and it had allowed me to book at the last minute. And now apparently so had Sadie.

It took me a second to recognize her, she had on a long blonde wig that mimicked her own hair back in the day. She must have decided to come incognito. Just exactly what was she planning?

We hugged for a very long time.

"I can't believe you're here. Thanks for coming." I swept the happy tears from my cheeks with my fingers. Sadie's had welled up as well. Though there was nobody nearby, we kept our voices low.

"I couldn't let you face this alone, bestie. I knew what you were going to do after that last phone call when you reminded me where your will was located. You made the excuse it was because of what happened to Rose today and the fire, but I saw right through it. I realized you would sacrifice yourself to keep the rest of us safe. To provide for us."

"Was Ashley okay when you left her? Is she at Riverbend?"

Sadie nodded, the blonde hair dancing on her shoulders. She looked so much like her former self I almost called her Merri. "Rose's family is settling in well too, far as I could tell. I couldn't stay long or I would have missed my flight. She promised to feed and walk Andy."

"Thank you. Was she buying my excuse of having to be in Toronto for an important meeting about my new app, and that it couldn't be delayed because they were traveling internationally? It was the only opportunity to meet them face to face?"

"I think so. But you know Rose, she has quite the need for having her say. She said you'd better be bringing her and the kids back some good souvenirs. She was a little hurt, I think, but it's not like you had much choice.

You're fighting to keep a roof over her head, for heaven's sake. A roof you bought and paid for and now that snake in the grass is trying to steal. Brad disgusts me," she hissed. "Makes me want to wring his bloody neck."

"No more than me. But much as I want to push him overboard, I can't do it in good conscience. It has to be something else. Something incriminating so he'll leave me alone." I rubbed my aching forehead at the monumental task still left to accomplish.

"He's here with Willow Sullivan, right? What if we set him up? Take incriminating photos of him while he's passed out? The Sullivans are not the type to put up with him making them look bad. I'm certain there were some words after the Costco incident that probably resulted in you getting Andy back."

"I could live with that. But how are we going to get him to pass out."

"Ashley lent me this." Sadie held up a small vial between her fingers I recognized. "Men have been doing it to women for decades."

"I know," I hedged. "But not sure I can do that. I don't want to be in the same category as people who do that."

"Well, do you have a better idea?" Sadie looked disappointed by my reluctance.

"Sorry, I know you're only trying to help. I just got to get my mind around it."

"He's threatening all you have, Katie. Your ability to make a living, your home, your very freedom. And not just yours, but mine and Ashley's, and now Rose's family. What more does he have to do for you to take action?"

I knew Sadie was right. Brad had acted deplorably. Long as he had the upper hand, everything that mattered to me was in peril. I just couldn't let this go, so why was I reluctant to act? Maybe I was just tired of it all, but I must stand and fight.

"I know you're right. But we would need the opportunity. How are we going to manage that? He's going to be suspicious."

"He won't recognize me in this wig, more makeup, and a short tight dress. I'll pretend to seduce him, ask him back to my cabin where you'll be waiting. After I put it in his drink, we set him up. Males have been getting away with it for years, or at least until recently. It's not rocket science."

I gave a snort. "Thanks. When you put it like that, seems almost too easy."

"Let's hope it is." I looked around to make certain no one was paying us any attention. Seemed the few people on deck had vanished during our conversation except for two men. One I instantly recognized. "Shush, don't look now, but Brad's over there."

The pair of us weren't visible to the two men standing near the rail, disguised as we were behind a couple of taller deck chairs and a potted palm.

The voices got louder. They were arguing about something or other. My tinnitus was getting in the way of hearing clearly. It would take many stress-free days to bring it under control.

"Do you know the other guy?" Sadie whispered.

I shook my head. "No."

"They're arguing about money. The guy wants money from Brad. Some of the cash he just won."

"Good luck on trying to get any of that." I scoffed. "Brad is notoriously tight-fisted. I once suggested he see a therapist about it. Oh, darn it, that reminds me, I forgot to cancel my own appointment this morning. Now I'll have to pay for that as well." It seemed rather insignificant in light of things.

"You do something about that bastard and you won't need a therapist," Sadie said, cocking an eyebrow.

She looked so focused, much better than she had in years. This vendetta against my ex was agreeing with her. Go figure.

"Maybe we should go into business getting justice for women taken advantage of by their ex?" I suggested with a forced grin.

"I wouldn't go that far. But it feels good to help you, Katie. You saved my life all those years ago. It's something you never forget."

The past flooded back in, making me wince with pain. The residue pain from the shallow bullet wound was nothing compared to the pain in my heart. "But I didn't save Josie's."

"No one could. You did your best by me. I didn't make it easy. I knew Wyatt had issues, was abusive, I could have left sooner." Her confession eased some of my guilt.

I touched her arm. "You didn't know what could happen, it's not your fault or mine. It's time we quit beating ourselves up, bestie."

"See, I was right, you don't need a therapist anymore." Sadie brushed the tears from her eyes, smiling through the sadness. It was a good moment for her, I could see she was trying. I prayed she was on the road to truly healing. I would do everything in my power to make that happen.

I glanced over at the men again, realizing the argument was not only continuing, but had escalated. An actual physical fight had broken out. Both men appeared drunk, pushing and shoving each other.

"What should we do?"

Sadie shrugged. "Nothing. Let them fight it out. Maybe we'll get lucky and one of them will end up overboard, never to be seen again."

"I should be so lucky. My karma has been askew for years."

CHAPTER 37
KATIE

WEDNESDAY 12:59 A.M.

We did not get that lucky, of course. Sadie headed off to bed when the pair of drunken idiots finally stopped fighting. I lingered on deck, going over the plan in my head that Sadie and I had agreed upon. It did have a chance at succeeding. I'd give it fifty-fifty at most, but at least that was something.

I stared at the moon, wishing I was that young girl again who believed anything was possible, that people were mostly good. Brad had made me doubt that, stopped me from growing in so many ways. But tonight, things had gotten better between Sadie and me, something I was grateful for. Resolve the problem with my ex and maybe the future could be brighter. All of us living at Riverbend would be about the best outcome of all.

"What are you doing here?" Suddenly Brad was in my face again. He looked worse for the wear. I thought he might sport a black eye in the morning, judging by the bruising near one eye. Not that he could feel that judging by the alcohol fumes surrounding him. He had a champagne bottle clutched in one hand. He took a big swig from it now, some dribbling down his chin. Not a good look.

"Nothing much. Watching a pair of morons fight over money." I tugged my sweater tighter around my body and turned to leave.

"You think you're better than me?" Brad stood in my way now, looming over me.

"No." I moved to step around him.

"You're a fucking murderer. I could have you arrested just like that." He snapped his fingers. "Maybe I need to make you pay for that in another way? Seems I got all the power now." His expression turned lecherous and my heart sank. The only thing worse than a sober Brad was a drunken one. It had been passion and sex that had led to our relationship in the first place. A blunder of gigantic proportions on my part.

"You're in my way. Move."

"Not until I get something for my trouble, sugar." Sugar. That old nickname that Brad had called me during our courtship and hasty marriage, standing for how sweet I was to him. Or at least, had been.

"Not going to happen." I stood my ground. "Not if you were the last man on earth."

"You doth protest too much, sugar. What's one more roll in the hay, to seal our deal? Willow need never know. She's sound asleep with another one of her famous headaches. You two have one thing in common unfortunately. Face it, you owe me, and you always will." His gloating rankled my last nerve. How dare he demand sex to keep me quiet!

"Let me get this right. You want Riverbend, all my earnings for the foreseeable future, and now sex on demand." I shook my head. "When did you turn into this person? How I could have seen anything in you, defies reason. Get out of my way, you cheating bastard!"

I went to push past him and he grabbed my wrist, twisting it painfully. "You think you're better than me, think again."

"Brad, what are you doing?" Willow asked, suddenly right there in our personal space. Her expression was dismayed, obviously shocked at how awful the man she was currently with was treating his ex. "I come up on deck for some fresh air and I find you accosting Katie? Demanding sex for you to stay quiet. What the hell is going on?"

"Oops, sorry, sweetheart, it's all a misunderstanding. I was just teasing. Of course, I don't want anything from Katie. What are you doing here? I thought you had a bad headache?" He let go of my wrist. I stood and rubbed it, the bones aching from being abused.

"It didn't look like that! You were pressuring her for sex. That's disgusting! And to think I came here to help you celebrate your win."

Wow. I didn't see Willow taking my side in this. She jabbed a finger into his chest and he winced, moving backward.

"I'll leave you two to talk." I sidestepped the pair, intending to head to my cabin.

"Katie's not who you think she is," Brad was protesting. "She murdered a guy last night."

"If he was anything like you, I could see why!"

Oh boy, looked like that relationship was well and truly over. Seducing Brad was looking to be easier than I'd thought. Then a terrible realization overcame me. But if it didn't matter anymore, because he was breaking up with Willow, what would it matter if we got those incriminating photos? They'd have to be really bad now to make any dent or difference to his lifestyle.

Willow was now screaming at Brad. I turned for a second to glance back at the pair from the top of the staircase I was about to descend. They were backed up far too close to the rail for comfort. I wanted to shout, *be careful*. Somehow Willow had gotten the champagne bottle away from Brad and in a split second she hit him over the head with it. He slumped sideways onto the rail. I stood there, uncertain of what to do next. Should I go back? Help? Memories of all the guilt I had carried for years flooded back. There was no other choice, I had to intervene.

"Willow, don't do it! You'll just trap yourself in guilt."

I rushed forward. I had to stop another woman from enduring the pain of guilt.

Willow looked at me as I skidded to a stop a few feet away. Her face was a study in anger, frustration, and pure betrayal. I knew all too well how what she was undergoing.

"I understand. But he's not worth it. You'll just dig a hole for yourself too deep to get out of."

Brad held his head, looking too dazed to deal with things. He most likely had a bad concussion. Blood was pouring down his face. If I hadn't hardened my heart against him, I might feel sorry for the bastard. But it was all left up to me now. If I could just save one more woman from a lifetime of regret, I'd say whatever it took to help her see reason.

"Please, walk away. Take the high road. I beg you."

"That bastard deserves to get his." She was shaking with emotion, but she wasn't holding a gun.

"He will. Plaster this around social media and he'll get his comeuppance. Or write a country and western song. That's a long-admired way to get even with a cheating ex."

Willow gave a shaky laugh. "I'm musically challenged."

"You got lots of money, right? Hire someone to write one. Or maybe you'd like in on a little scheme that Sadie and I are planning?" The last bit spilled out without thinking, but I did say it a little quieter, just in case Brad was better off than he looked.

She came closer, and I breathed a sigh of relief. Yes. Crisis averted, for her, anyway. The outcome for me was still up in the air.

Our arms around each other, supporting us and keeping us from keeling over, I could feel how much she was still trembling. We left Brad to his own devices. I had one dark moment when I kind of wanted to boot him off the deck and into the dark water below, but I managed to contain myself.

On the way down to Willow's cabin I explained my plan B at her insistence.

"I like it. I'll give you a hand."

And so, she did, facilitating it by pretending to forgive Brad and letting him back into the cabin. By the time Sadie and I left the cruise, we had all become friends. Willow stayed on board, wanting to see more of Alaska. Brad left in a huff after we showed him what we had on him. It wasn't good. Suffice it to say he looked smashing in a ball gag and strategically placed leather strapping, or at least I would imagine his competitors would think so if they ever got their hands on the incriminating evidence. Maybe not murder, but evidence of his watching snuff films was close enough. Seemed Willow Sullivan had the money to buy most anything, an enemy one should be careful not to make. I'd bear that in mind going forward.

EPILOGUE

KATIE

FOUR YEARS LATER

I grabbed my phone just as it was about to topple into
our backyard pool, vibrating on the glass table I had set
it on earlier, making it dance too close to the edge. It
had been a rare, lazy day lying about on my lounger
catching a few rays to disguise my pasty skin after the
long prairie winter. Riverbend had remained quiet, just
Andy and me for the past few hours while Rose and her
crew went grocery shopping for the May long weekend.
Sadie was spending the day with her new boyfriend
Daniel Johnson from across the street. Now that was a
good sign, Sadie spending time with a man again, even if
he was considerably older than her. But maybe she
needed someone with a better understanding of the
world that only experience can bring. Fingers crossed
for her. That whole situation with the police had
evolved into a cold case, with suspects unknown. It
could just stay like that, in my opinion. Not like my ex
was going to say anything anytime soon. The cruise

fiasco had effectively silenced him. *Thank you, Willow Sullivan.* We'd stayed in touch, and I found I liked her company more than expected, though I'd always be a little on guard around her.

The number that had popped up on my phone was familiar and I answered the call with pleasure. Ashley. She'd gone on after that terrible experience that we all tried to keep desperately from haunting us, to become an excellent mother to Lily, a feisty little girl that we all adored. I loved being an honorary aunt to Lily as much as I enjoyed being an aunt to Meghan, Tess, and Joe Junior. But Ashley's daughter would always have a special place in my heart. And in Sadie's. Somehow it eased our losing Josie, making sure Ashley's little girl grew up in a safe, loving environment.

The pair of them had stayed on at Riverbend, Ashley acquiring her early learning and childcare provider certificate to be with her daughter while she worked. For the past couple of years, she had been taking courses toward her education degree and hoped to become a teacher in an elementary school one day. She'd lived common law with Isaac Bello for the eighteen months now, moving out of Riverbend to live with him near the University of Manitoba where he was a teaching assistant. She seemed happy and excited about the future, and that's all any of us wanted for her and Lily. Isaac had taken the pair of them home to Nigeria to meet his family a few months ago, and his relatives, especially his mother, had been very welcoming. She'd even asked for them to come back soon and Ashley and Isaac were considering going back at Christmas, though Ashley was dragging her heels, saying she didn't want to go there yet and spend so much money.

"Hey, Ashley."

"Katie! I don't know what I'm going to do. I'm in terrible trouble."

Ashley's words rushed over themselves. A shiver of fear snaked down my spine. I sat up straighter, hanging on her every word.

"Slow down. What is it? What's wrong?"

"It's Lily. Isaac was trying to take her away from me. He said he was sick of the cold winters in Canada and our fighting lately about our going back to Nigeria at Christmas. I told him last night that he had to move out, that I was sick of all the fighting, that it wasn't good for Lily. He didn't take it well, threatened me, slammed me against the wall before walking out. Said I would live to regret it. Then today he had my daughter clutched in his hands when I came home early unexpectedly. Said he was taking Lily to his mother who always wanted a daughter. Lily was crying and trying to get away. I hit him, really, really hard, with a rolling pin. It was lying on the counter because Lily and I were going to bake some chocolate chip cookies later. I think he's dead. Oh my god! What am I going to do?"

I got up from the lounger as she spoke, unable to sit still while I took in the situation. I asked the most important question, my heart in my throat. "Is Lily okay?"

"Yes, I think so, poor baby. She's in her bedroom right now, watching her favorite cartoons on my iPad."

"I'm coming right over. We can fix this. Don't move and *don't* call the police, not until I get there. Okay?" And definitely not then either. Last thing we needed was to involve the law and have Lily taken into foster care, even if just for a few days until this was sorted. The scars from events like that stayed forever. I would know, after all the stories that Ashley had shared with me these past few years about her terrible experiences caught up in the system. Most defied description, turning my stomach into a raw war zone.

"I won't. Just come quick."

"Don't worry. Aunt Katie will make this right, no matter what it takes."

Now that was a promise I could make without reservation. Like my grandmother before me liked to say, *you're never given more than you can handle, child.* Turns out my mission in life was providing safety to loved ones. I could handle that load now. Not like I hadn't had a lot of practice. And Riverbend was a large property after all. Best part, I had found the courage to forgive myself for only doing what I've been called upon to do. Doesn't get better than that.

After all, no good deed goes unpunished as they like to say.

A LOOK AT: NO ORDINARY MAN

A man with a frightening skill set, a drug kingpin looking to use him to expand his influence, and the woman caught in the middle.

A lightning strike has left Jackson Banks scarred both inside and out, gifting him the power to stop men in their tracks. This ability defies nature and has left his life in shambles after causing the death of his own mother.

With his past sins weighing him down, Jackson fears he's destined to be alone, a monster hiding in the shadows. But when his abilities are discovered by two Mexican drug cartels, he is forced into a life he could not have imagined, sparking a war between the cartels.

Caught in a deadly tug-of-war between power-hungry factions, Jackson finds unexpected solace in Elena, a woman who sees beyond his scars to the man he truly is. As their love ignites, so does the conflict, thrusting Jackson into a perilous showdown with his past and the sinister forces that seek to control him.

Will Jackson muster the courage to confront his demons and fight for a future with Elena?

AVAILABLE JUNE 2024

ABOUT THE AUTHOR

January Bain is an award-winning author who firmly believes that stories unite us, that good stories help us to discover the commonality of the human experience by supporting values, empathy and understanding. She writes with her heart, mind, and soul, hoping that her novels will touch your life, giving you moments of freedom as you fly with her to other worlds.

Bain has had the pleasure of select novels being turned into games, and her work is also available in different languages.

January and her husband live in rural Canada on peaceful acreage where a variety of wildlife comes to visit regularly and expect to be fed and paid attention to.